TALES FROM
SCHWARTZGARTEN

OSBERT
THE AVENGER

D0311299

For CJN

ORCHARD BOOKS
338 Euston Road, London NW1 3BH
Orchard Books Australia
Level 17/207 Kent Street, Sydney, NSW 2000

ISBN 978 1 40831 455 5

First published in hardback in Great Britain in 2012
This edition published in Great Britain in 2013
Text © Christopher William Hill 2012

A CIP catalogue record for this book is available
from the British Library.

10 9 8 7 6 5 4   (paperback)

Printed in Great Britain

Orchard Books is a division of Hachette Children's
Books, an Hachette UK company.

www.hachette.co.uk

Schwartzgarten map illustration by Artful Doodlers © Orchard Books 2012
The Informant illustrations © Chris Naylor 2012

TALES FROM
SCHWARTZGARTEN

OSBERT
THE AVENGER

Christopher William Hill

ORCHARD

THE CITY OF SCHWARTZGARTEN

CEMETERY

Bone Orchard Street

OLD TOWN

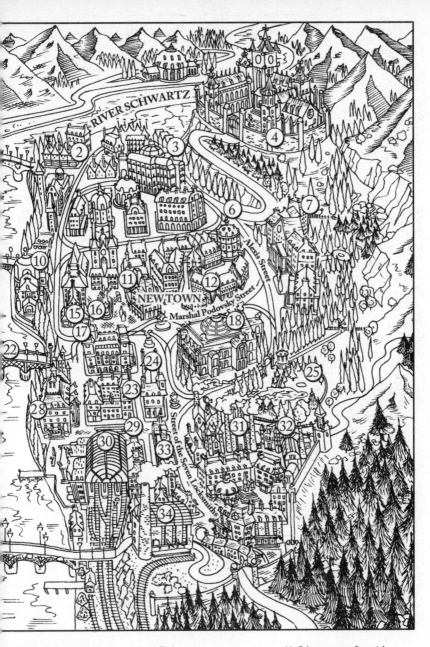

Chapter One

OSBERT BRINKHOFF was born on a Tuesday to a respectable family in an obscure corner of the city of Schwartzgarten. Mr and Mrs Brinkhoff, who had dreamed of rearing a genius, welcomed little Osbert's considerable breadth of skull and elevated forehead with undisguised glee.

'He has the head of an intellectual colossus,' observed Mr Brinkhoff.

'Indeed,' replied Doctor Zimmermann, eyeing the child with some suspicion as he packed away his forceps and stethoscope. 'I shouldn't be surprised if your little boy grows up to be the most intelligent citizen in the whole of this great city.'

And so it was that Osbert Brinkhoff's story began.

The Brinkhoff family lived in a comfortable apartment on Marshal Podovsky Street, close to the library and overlooking the greasy brown river that coiled like a serpent through the heart of Schwartzgarten.

Mr Brinkhoff worked as a middle-ranking clerk at the Bank of Muller, Baum and Spink and had far more ambition for his son than he had ever had for himself. Even so, his own prospects were excellent, and it had been decided that when the ancient Mr Spink finally expired, the bank's name would be changed to Muller, Baum and Brinkhoff.

Mrs Brinkhoff was very proud of her husband, whom she adored. She would lie in bed at night and pray that Mr Muller and Mr Baum would die in a terrible accident, so that when Osbert was old enough he and Mr Brinkhoff could run the bank all by themselves.

But as the years passed and Osbert grew into a little boy, he showed no inclination towards banking. He was always small for his age, with pale skin and intense blue eyes. He had inherited his father's poor eyesight, and wore spectacles from his earliest years. He did not want to play with other children, but would instead sit for hours in his bedroom, reading books on physics and algebra that he had taken from his father's study, pushing a chair under the doorknob so that he would not be disturbed.

This was not quite the boy the Brinkhoffs had dreamt of. Finally, in desperation, they decided they had no choice but to engage the services of a nanny to look after Osbert, in the hope that she could prevent the boy from becoming irredeemably peculiar. Turning to the 'Home Help' section of *The Schwartzgarten Daily Examiner* on the eve of Osbert's sixth birthday, they found a small advertisement that seemed to answer their prayers: *Boys taken care of, no questions asked. Over thirty years' experience.*

———

On the day Nanny arrived, the sky turned a curious shade of mauve. The weather was warm and suffocating, and as Nanny hauled herself up the steps to the Brinkhoff apartment, Osbert watched her suspiciously from his bedroom window. Nanny was a large woman, almost spherical. She was dressed in black from head to toe: black boots, black skirt, black coat and black feathers sticking upright from her large black hat.

'Like an overfed raven,' thought Osbert, grimly.

Mr and Mrs Brinkhoff met with Nanny in the study and Osbert listened at the keyhole.

'You will find that Osbert is a very clever boy,' observed Mr Brinkhoff, the pride in his voice tinged with anxiety. 'But as with all clever boys, he must be watched very closely.'

The armchair in which Nanny sat groaned under her great weight as she leant forward, eyeing the Brinkhoffs with a steely gaze. 'The thing about boys,' she whispered mysteriously, 'even the oddest of them can become quite normal again. It's like gorillas in the zoo,' she rasped, and Mrs Brinkhoff coughed nervously. 'Little boys must be *tamed*.'

The following day, Nanny awoke early in her apartment in the Old Town. She packed two suitcases, switched off the gas and electricity and covered the furniture with large white dust cloths. Securely locking the door of the apartment, she made her way downstairs and out onto Donmerplatz, where she caught the tram across the city to take up her new position in the home of the Brinkhoff family.

Mrs Brinkhoff thought it best that Nanny should settle into her new home before being introduced to little Osbert. But little Osbert had other ideas. As Nanny unpacked her suitcases, she became aware of the fact that she was no longer alone. There, in the doorway, stood Osbert, observing her every move.

'So you are little Osbert Brinkhoff?' said Nanny.

Gravely, Osbert nodded his head.

'Do you have a kiss for Nanny?'

Osbert shook his head.

'Suit yourself,' said Nanny and continued unpacking her bags.

Osbert watched from the door with growing curiosity as Nanny opened a case and took out a dozen silver picture frames, wrapped carefully in tissue paper. She unwrapped the pictures and placed them on the chest of drawers. The largest of the frames she positioned on the table beside her bed.

Tentatively, Osbert entered the room. He stared hard at the photograph on the bedside table.

'Marshal Potemkin,' explained Nanny. 'My first love. Poisoned to death.'

Osbert moved to survey the photographs on the chest of drawers.

'General Metzger,' continued Nanny, 'killed by a bomb the day before our wedding…and beside him, Marshal Beckmann, who had his head chopped off by a cutlass… Ah, how I loved Marshal Beckmann.' Nanny sighed, wistfully. 'Dead. All dead.'

Twelve photographs of twelve celebrated military leaders, all beloved by Nanny until they had met their grisly ends.

'So I never married,' said Nanny. 'None of them lived long enough.' She smiled. 'And that's why I turned to nannying.'

———◆———

Nanny was used to little boys. In her thirty-year career she had seen most types of child imaginable: the sort that shouted and spat, the sort that fidgeted and moped, even the sort that bullied and lied. But Osbert was something different. He was watchful and intelligent.

This unsettled Nanny. The key, she decided, to taming the boy, was to remain eternally vigilant.

But Osbert had no intention of being tamed, no matter how hard Nanny tried. She would tie him to a chair and refuse to release him until he'd eaten all his supper, but Osbert would always wriggle free. She would threaten him with monsters under the bed, but it would only disappoint him when the monsters failed to materialise. She would dose the boy with cod liver oil, only to find that Osbert had returned the favour by adding the oil to Nanny's cup of cocoa.

As the weeks passed, Osbert became sick of Nanny's attempts to tame him. One day, while his keeper was out, he tiptoed into her bedroom. He was in search of clues; clues to prove that Nanny was not to be trusted with the care of a young and impressionable genius. As he began opening the chest of drawers he was certain he would find evidence of wrongdoing. At first he could find nothing but raven-feather hats in various stages of decrepitude and half-eaten packets of salted caramels.

But then, as his fingers felt around the corners of the final drawer, he discovered a false bottom had been added. Carefully lifting the wooden panel, he found wires and putty, an alarm clock timer, a rusted cutlass and a green glass bottle decorated with a skull and crossbones.

'Do unto others before they can do unto you,' said a voice.

Osbert turned and there stood Nanny. She took the wooden panel from Osbert and carefully replaced it at the bottom of the drawer, covering over the treasure trove of Nanny's 'hidden things'.

Osbert smiled. Life had suddenly become interesting.

'Our little secret,' said Nanny, and Osbert crossed his heart.

———✦———

Something had changed. It seemed that Nanny had a grudging respect for Osbert, and in turn Osbert had a new-found respect for Nanny.

'I'm loyal to the families I work for, Osbert,' said Nanny. 'People that treat me good get goodness back. I'd maim or kill for my families if I had to.'

'And have you had to?' asked Osbert, burning with curiosity.

'That's for me to know,' said Nanny, tapping the side of her nose with a stubby finger. 'But let's just say there's them in their graves that got there earlier than nature intended.'

As time passed, Nanny grew fond of Osbert. He could be a kind and thoughtful boy, and would sometimes read her mathematical calculations that he thought she might find amusing from his book of algebra.

Osbert and Nanny would go on long walks together: along Marshal Podovsky Street, past the Governor's Palace with its green copper dome and on into Edvardplatz, where they would stand and watch the great clock striking the hour. Sometimes they would walk out onto the Grand Duke Augustus Bridge, gazing down as the foaming water surged beneath them. As Osbert grew older their walks would take them further – across the Princess Euphenia Bridge and into the Old Town beyond. Osbert was fascinated by the Old Town. The buildings seemed darker, the streets were narrower and everywhere hung the noxious fumes from the glue factory.

'You see up there?' said Nanny, pointing to a window on the seventh floor of a decrepit apartment block. 'That's where I used to live.'

'I don't like it,' said Osbert.

'It's not so bad,' said Nanny, 'if you don't mind the stench from the glue factory, and you're happy to chance a desperate cutthroat creeping in and slicing you from ear to ear while you're tucked up in sleepy-land.' She gave a gurgling laugh, like water escaping down the plughole.

Osbert disliked the place intensely and Nanny could feel his shiver as she tightly held his hand.

'There's somewhere I think you *would* like to see,' said Nanny, as she walked with Osbert to the end of the street. Crossing over long abandoned tramlines they encountered a high, grey wall, which seemed to extend forever in both directions.

'They call this Bone-Orchard Street,' said Nanny, with a dark twinkle in her eye. 'We go left here.'

After walking for over ten minutes, the wall parted at a monumental gateway.

'The Gate of Skulls,' whispered Nanny in awe.

Looking up, Osbert saw that the gateway was topped by a pyramid of iron skulls. Sitting atop this grisly mound was an ornamental skeleton in black robes and a golden crown, his bony finger outstretched and pointing to the path below.

'Look,' said Nanny, her breath hot and sticky with excitement. 'He's pointing at us. You and me. They could be our skulls he's sitting on.'

Beyond the gates lay the Schwartzgarten Municipal Cemetery. Although Osbert had never visited the cemetery before, he knew its reputation well. The city of Schwartzgarten had been blighted by over two hundred years of civil unrest, bloody sieges, battles and political assassinations. This, of course, had resulted in a vast quantity of bodies, all in need of burial. The cemetery was a quarter of the size of Schwartzgarten itself, and was known by many as 'the Dark City'.

Nanny bought twelve white roses from the cemetery flower seller and led Osbert in through the Gate of Skulls. They left the central avenue, which led through the heart of the cemetery, and continued along a narrower, darker path, in the shade of a row of yew trees. When it seemed the path could get no darker, Nanny and Osbert rounded a corner and stepped out into a bright, paved courtyard. The sun was low in the sky, but the rays of light were reflected off the grand tombs of white marble that lined the square. It was like moonlight in the middle of the day. Nanny turned slowly, staring hard at the carved and gleaming busts that topped each and every one of the twelve tombs in the courtyard. The faces looked familiar to Osbert; they were military men with neatly trimmed beards and elaborately twirled moustaches.

'My darlings,' Nanny whispered. 'My dear, dead darlings.'

Inside the twelve tombs were interred the mortal remains of Nanny's lost loves: General Metzger, Marshal Beckmann and the rest.

'Do unto others before they can do unto you,' said Osbert gravely.

Nanny flashed him a wicked smile and placed a white rose at the foot of each tomb, finally laying a bloom at the carved feet of Marshal Potemkin.

'My first and greatest love of all,' whispered Nanny, kissing the Marshal's cold stone face. 'Such a brave soldier. Drank down a whole bottle of cyanide in his beetroot schnapps, and not a word of complaint.'

Although Nanny was happy to educate Osbert in the ways of the world, relating dark tales of intrigue and murder, she left the boy's formal education to his parents. And so, throughout his early childhood, Mr and Mrs Brinkhoff tutored Osbert at home; Mrs Brinkhoff during the day and Mr Brinkhoff when he returned from the bank each evening. But as he reached his eleventh birthday it became clear that they were no longer equal to the challenge of educating their son – he was simply too clever for them. He could carry out long division in moments, memorise extensive tracts of poetry after just one reading and would discuss the history of Schwartzgarten as if he himself had borne witness to its long and exceptionally bloody past.

'There is only one thing for it,' whispered Mr

Brinkhoff to his wife, as he prised a book of algebra from the arms of his sleeping son. 'He must sit the entrance exam for The Institute.'

'He can't,' said Mrs Brinkhoff, shaking her head. 'He mustn't.'

'I don't like it any more than you do,' said Mr Brinkhoff sadly, 'but the boy is too clever for us. Too clever by far. If he's accepted into The Institute, who knows what he might achieve?'

Mrs Brinkhoff shuddered and tucked Osbert into bed, kissing him gently on his great forehead. She feared the worst: The Institute would take her son from her, and who knew what would happen next?

CHAPTER TWO

———◆◆◆◆◆———

THE INSTITUTE was built on a high hill in the northernmost reaches of the city, and its towering walls of slate-grey stone could be seen from most of the apartments and houses in Schwartzgarten. It was a chilling building; it struck fear into the hearts of all who gazed upon it, and not without due reason. Even the school inspectors refused to visit The Institute, and would instead write from time to time, inquiring after the welfare of the children, making certain that they were all still alive.

The Institute selected only the most intelligent children from the city, and every year they would invite applications from prospective students. With a heavy heart, Mr Brinkhoff sat down at his study desk and wrote to Mr Rudulfus, the Deputy Principal of The Institute and Master of Admissions, inquiring if his son could be considered for a place at the beginning of the new academic term.

A week later a letter arrived, banded in black and addressed to Osbert. The letter read as follows:

Osbert Brinkhoff, do you really imagine you have what it takes to become a scholar at The Institute? What makes you think you stand a chance of admission when your father failed his own entrance exam so miserably? Examinations will be held on the third day of next month. If you expect to fail, as your father before you, do not bother to attend.

The letter was signed in a barely legible and inky scrawl, *The Principal*.

Osbert ran to his father's study and showed him the mysterious letter. 'Is it true, Father?' inquired Osbert. '*Did* you fail your entrance exam?'

Mr Brinkhoff stood sadly at the window, staring out across the city to the distant hills on which The Institute was perched like a mighty and diabolical gargoyle.

'At last you know the truth,' said Mr Brinkhoff, who had always known that his failure would one day come to light. 'I did not pass my examination. They said my answers were too whimsical.' He sighed whimsically, and patted Osbert on the shoulder. This was not true of course; all Mr Brinkhoff had ever heard from The Institute was deafening silence. 'But you, my boy,' he continued, smiling proudly, 'you have a real chance of being accepted.'

Day after day, night after night, Osbert worked at the desk in his father's study, preparing for his entrance exam. Mr Brinkhoff was a patient tutor and sat with his son for hours at a time, quizzing him on algebra and Latin, physics and history. He was determined that Osbert would not endure the same crushing humiliation that he had suffered so many years before.

———

The day of the examination dawned. Mrs Brinkhoff, who could not look at her son without weeping, sat quietly in the sitting room while Nanny cut rounds of raisin bread, thinly sliced and thickly buttered, for Osbert to eat on his journey to The Institute.

It was a bitterly cold morning, and Mr Brinkhoff held his son firmly by the hand as he led him along the treacherously icy pavement. As the bell rang and the tram rattled into view, Mr Brinkhoff's grip tightened on Osbert's hand.

The tram hurtled dangerously along the banks of the River Schwartz, and Mr Brinkhoff continued to prepare his son for the impending entrance exam, reciting mathematical equations and Latin verse.

As they lurched past Edvardplatz and the Governor's Palace, Mr Brinkhoff secretly thought of ringing the bell to stop the rackety vehicle, running back home with Osbert and securely bolting the door behind them. But as they rounded a corner and the high, dark walls of The Institute became visible once more above the shops and apartments, he knew that it was too late. Whatever would be, would be.

The tramlines stopped at the bottom of the hill that led to The Institute, so Osbert and Mr Brinkhoff completed their journey by foot. The road was steep, and for a while the school seemed to completely disappear beyond the brow of the hill. On they walked, slipping from time to time on the frozen cobbles, and as they finally crested the hill The Institute suddenly loomed back into view.

Observed from a distance it was a miserable building, but close up it appeared even more bleak and foreboding. Perched at the top of the towering grey walls, three large stone gargoyles leered out across the city. A fourth gargoyle had toppled from the roof many years before and crashed into the roof of the gymnasium, where it remained, lodged in the ceiling, one of its enormous stone wings protruding through the tiles.

There was only one entrance to The Institute, and this was through an ornate pair of wrought-iron gates set into the high wall that surrounded the building. Above the gates, in gilt lettering, was the Latin maxim, *Scientia est potentia*.

'And do you know what the phrase means?' asked Mr Brinkhoff.

'Yes, Father,' replied Osbert, who was quickly mastering the dead language of Latin, 'it means "Knowledge is Power".'

On the wall beside the gates was a bell pull and an engraved brass plaque. *For attention, ring bell. Students only.*

Summoning up his courage, Mr Brinkhoff rang the bell.

A small door opened in the wall just beyond the gates, and a man barely taller than Osbert appeared, weighed down by an enormous bundle of keys that was chained to his belt.

'Can't you read?' he hissed. 'Students only. Don't want every fool ringing the bell, it'll wear out.'

'My name is Mr Brinkhoff,' said Mr Brinkhoff, 'and this is my son, Osbert.'

'You're expected,' said the Porter. 'You'd better come in.'

'Thank you,' replied Mr Brinkhoff, removing his hat.

'Not you,' hissed the Porter. 'The boy.' He unlocked the gates and ushered Osbert inside.

'As you know, Osbert,' Mr Brinkhoff began, 'I am very proud of everything you—'

'No time for all that,' said the Porter impatiently. 'We haven't got all day.'

Osbert stepped forward and the Porter pushed the gates shut behind them, turning the key in the lock.

Mr Brinkhoff smiled encouragingly through the railings. 'Good luck. I shall wait here until you've finished your examination.'

'Follow me,' said the Porter, beckoning to Osbert with a stiff, arthritic finger.

He led the boy across the central courtyard, around which the grey slate walls of the school rose steeply, seeming almost to obliterate the sky above. The Institute's only windows looked out over the courtyard; the windows which once faced out towards the city had been bricked up long before, to prevent students becoming distracted from their lessons by life beyond the school.

In the centre of the courtyard stood a monumental alabaster statue of The Institute's founder, the late Julius Offenbach, who had run the school with an iron fist, until he met with a slow and painful end, boiling to death in his own bathtub. Some said it had been a terrible accident, but many others argued that it hadn't been an accident at all, and that Offenbach's screams of pain had simply been ignored by the children of The Institute.

Osbert found it impossible to make out the face of the statue, covered as it was by a skin of thick green moss. One arm, which originally held a cane (to serve as a warning to the students as they entered The Institute each morning) had been struck by lightning years before, crashing to the ground and shattering into many thousands of pieces. No longer was there grass in the courtyard, but the hardiest weeds climbed the slate walls that surrounded it, seemingly choking the life out of the school itself.

High above and to the left of the courtyard, a tiny window looked out over the school. Osbert glanced up, and thought he saw a dark figure step back from the glass.

'Don't look unless you're told to look,' snapped the Porter, his pace suddenly quickening.

Beyond the courtyard, a large green door loomed before them, and it was through this door that the Porter beckoned Osbert. 'This way.'

The corridor was dark and musty.

'Haven't got all day,' said the Porter.

To begin with, Osbert had to feel his way along the dark gas-lit passageway, until slowly his eyes became accustomed to the gloom.

'Don't dawdle, boy,' muttered the Porter, quickening

his step once more as a large hall clock struck the quarter-hour.

The Institute seemed even larger to Osbert than it had appeared from the outside. On and on he hurried, struggling to keep pace with his mumbling and bad-tempered guide.

Finally, at the end of a particularly dark stretch of corridor, they arrived at a door.

'In here,' grunted the Porter.

After the narrow confines of the dark passageways, nothing could have prepared Osbert for the cavernous dimensions of The Institute's gymnasium. Every footstep he took on the polished wooden floor echoed back sharply from the oak-panelled walls.

'Why don't you make *more* of a racket?' said the Porter sarcastically.

At the far end of the gymnasium was a stage with red velvet curtains, above which a large clock marked the passing seconds, the deep rumble of the clockwork mechanism beating as if it were the very heart of The Institute. A Latin inscription had been painted in Gothic lettering around the clock face:

SI HOC LEGERE SCIS NIMIUM

ERUDITIONIS HABES.

Osbert could only make out the words dimly through the lenses of his spectacles. The Porter was already hissing under his breath and beckoning Osbert forward. He pointed to a solitary desk and chair.

'But where are the other children?' asked Osbert.

'Only you and her,' said the Porter, nodding his head towards the opposite end of the hall. 'Only two at a time.'

Beneath a large oil painting of a three-headed dragon biting the head off a fat schoolboy, entitled *Knowledge Devouring Innocence*, there was another desk and chair that Osbert had failed to notice. Sitting at the desk was the most beautiful girl he had ever seen. Her skin was porcelain-white and even at a distance he could tell that her large, round eyes were a rare emerald green.

Osbert smiled and the Porter poked him with his finger.

'Sit down.'

Osbert took his seat.

'There's paper on the desk. Turn over the question

sheet as soon as you hear the old bell ring, not before. You'll have one hour exactly.'

'Then what will happen?' asked Osbert.

'Then I'll come to get you, won't I?' sneered the Porter. 'That's if you haven't been crushed to death first.'

He pointed to the ceiling and Osbert looked up. Protruding through the plaster were two legs and a wing of the fallen stone gargoyle, immediately above his desk.

'That's something to occupy your mind, isn't it?' grinned the Porter, as he clattered back across the polished floor and disappeared through the door.

Osbert wanted to turn around in his chair to gaze at the beautiful girl with the green eyes, but instead he sat silently in the vast, empty room, waiting for the bell to ring. And all the time he waited, he could sense that someone was watching him.

The minute hand on the gymnasium clock reached twelve, and from the very bowels of the building Osbert heard the tolling of an ancient bell. The noise seemed to rumble through the labyrinthine corridors of The Institute before bursting in through the door of the gymnasium.

Osbert attempted to appear calm as he turned over his exam paper.

Question one. Osbert Brinkhoff, do you really think you are a suitable candidate for The Institute? Are you prepared to be humiliated, the way your father was before you? If the answer is no, place your pen on the table and leave the gymnasium immediately.

Osbert could not quite believe what he was reading. He looked up from his desk and was sure he saw the velvet curtains of the stage twitch. Slowly, carefully, Osbert unscrewed the lid of his fountain pen and began to read question two, *Latin Comprehension*.

There was no doubt about it; somebody *was* watching him.

CHAPTER THREE

A MONTH AFTER Osbert's entrance examination, the new term began. There had been no communication from The Institute, no letter or telegram to suggest that Osbert's application had been successful, nor yet a sneering missive to dash the boy's hopes once and for all. And this was the way of things. It was not until the first day of the new term that the results were posted on the walls outside The Institute. Every aspect of this ritual was designed to be as inconvenient and humiliating as possible to the prospective candidates and their families. If the child had passed his or her exam, then the steep climb and the gnawing fear they'd experienced on their way to The Institute would all have been worthwhile. If, however, the child had been unsuccessful, they would find their name obliterated from the list with a neat line of red ink and would have nothing more to look forward to than the long journey back down the hill into the city.

The Schwartzgarten clock was still chiming eight as Osbert and Mr Brinkhoff hurried along Marshal Podovsky Street to the tram terminus. They made their journey in silence. Only when they stepped from the tram at the foot of the hill leading to The Institute did Mr Brinkhoff finally betray his emotions. His eye flickered as if in spasm and his hands began to tremble. They did not so much walk as run to the top of the hill, where already a large crowd of parents and children had gathered at the wrought-iron gates. It was a deeply unsettling sight. Osbert had never seen grown men cry. One man was clinging to the bars of the gates and had to be pulled away by his wife, who was almost choking as she inhaled her tears.

Carefully and apologetically, Mr Brinkhoff pushed his way to the front of the crowd, holding his son firmly by the hand. Peering through the railings, Osbert saw that the porcelain-pale girl with the green eyes was standing forlornly in the courtyard beyond the gates. Her mother was shouting words of encouragement from the crowd.

'I'm sure the stories aren't as bad as you've heard, my darling. I'm sure you'll be very happy.'

'Don't be *too* sure,' sneered the Porter. He turned and glowered through the bars at Osbert. 'Brinkhoff, is it? You're the wrong side of the gates.'

'You mean he passed his entrance exam?' whispered Mr Brinkhoff, hardly daring to believe that Osbert had been successful.

'Very good,' said the Porter, sarcastically. 'Brains must run in the family.'

Mr Brinkhoff fought his way to the notice-board beside the gates. There was the list of candidates: twenty names, eighteen of which had been neatly crossed through with red ink. Only two names remained unobliterated.

'*Osbert Brinkhoff,*' whispered Mr Brinkhoff, his stomach churning with a bewildering mix of pride and fear. He turned to Osbert. 'The Institute is only taking two new students this year.'

The Porter took the key from the chain around his waist and unlocked the gates. 'Get back,' he screamed as the most desperate parents in the crowd attempted to shove their unsuccessful and terrified children through the gates. 'Only him,' shouted the Porter. 'Only Osbert Brinkhoff.' He seized Osbert by the collar of his coat and dragged him through to the courtyard.

'I'll see you tonight,' shouted Mr Brinkhoff. 'Good luck!'

'He'll need it,' said the Porter, locking the gates securely.

Leaving the wailing crowds behind, Osbert turned to wave to his father.

'No waving,' said the Porter. 'It gives the parents hope when there is none.'

Osbert smiled at the girl with the green eyes. 'My name is Osbert Brinkhoff.'

The girl smiled back. 'I know,' she said. 'I'm Isabella Myop.'

'No talking,' screeched the Porter. 'Can't you read the signs?'

'But there aren't any signs,' said Isabella.

'And that's my fault, is it?' hissed the Porter. He left them at the doorway to The Institute and grinned unpleasantly. 'You're expected at nine o'clock sharp.

You know the way to the gymnasium.'

'But I've only been here once,' protested Isabella.

Ignoring the girl, the Porter turned on his heel and hurried back towards the gates, waving his fist angrily at the crowd.

Slowly, Osbert pushed open the enormous school door and, with Isabella at his side, entered the musty halls of The Institute.

———

It took Osbert and Isabella many minutes to negotiate their way along the dim, stale corridors. After what seemed like an eternity, they turned a corner that appeared strangely familiar. Pushing open the door at the end of this dark passageway, they found themselves at last in the gymnasium. Osbert glanced up at the clock above the stage, beating time mournfully in the great, empty hall. It was five past nine.

'We're late,' whispered Isabella, anxiously.

'Indeed you are,' replied a voice, unpleasantly.

Osbert and Isabella stared up at the stage, watching with mounting fear as the red velvet curtains swept open.

There, staring down at them, was a tall man, skeletally thin, dressed in a long black tailcoat.

'The Principal!' gasped Isabella. 'It must be!'

'Silence!' shrieked the man, his Malacca walking cane tapping rhythmically as he walked from the stage and descended the stairs into the hall.

Osbert and Isabella observed the man with trepidation. What little hair he had was a dirty orange, and it clung in greasy clumps to the sides of his head. His face looked unusually smooth for a man of his obvious great age and was marked only by an old fencing scar, which ran from his right cheekbone all the way down to his chin. He approached Osbert and Isabella, eyeing them both with what seemed like equal distrust. There was an unmistakable aroma of cough syrup and mustiness that seemed to hang about him. Close up, he looked even more skeletal than he did from a distance. It was like being in the presence of a living corpse.

'Your hair's too long,' spat the Principal, lifting Isabella's braids with his grey and bony fingers.

Osbert could see Isabella quiver with fear; he thought for a moment she might collapse in terror. But she did not.

'And you,' continued the Principal, poking Osbert in the stomach with the tip of his cane. 'Thought you were more intelligent than your father, eh? Well, we shall see.'

He tapped his cane on the polished wooden floor and a small man appeared from the back of the hall.

'Mr Lomm,' said the Principal, his eyes sparking with malevolent glee. 'You may now take your new students.'

Mr Lomm approached. Though a junior teacher, he had already earned a reputation for barbarity. Some even said that you could hear the screams from his students a hundred yards or more from his classroom door. Osbert, of course, did not believe the stories. But Isabella was not so certain.

Mr Lomm was round, with a pink face, and smelt of almond oil, which he used to plaster his dark hair into a shiny side parting. His alert brown eyes were framed by a pair of tortoiseshell spectacles. Were it not for the man's fearsome reputation, his face might even have been described as pleasant.

'Follow me,' snapped Mr Lomm. 'You're already late.'

The Principal's face contorted into a smile as Mr Lomm led Osbert and Isabella from the gymnasium.

They walked in silence along the dark corridors towards Mr Lomm's room. Osbert wanted to reach out his hand to Isabella, as much to calm his own fears as to comfort his new friend. But he knew this would not be allowed.

A voice bellowed from the darkness beyond, followed by a sharp yelp. A small girl shot out into the corridor in a cloud of sulphur vapours, like a cuckoo from a clock. She stopped suddenly, her movement arrested by a long plait of golden hair that coiled all the way back into the classroom.

'Good morning, Lomm,' came a woman's voice, as deep and low as a hippo.

'Good morning, Doctor Zilbergeld,' replied Mr Lomm. 'Punishing your students so early in the day, I see. Very good, very good.'

The golden-haired girl gave another shriek as Doctor Zilbergeld reeled the student back inside the chemistry classroom by her long plait, and the door slammed shut.

'This way,' said Mr Lomm as they continued along the passageway and turned a sharp corner. 'The West Wing.'

A disturbing noise seemed to curdle the air; it was the unmistakable sound of children screaming. Isabella stopped in her tracks.

'No dawdling,' snapped Mr Lomm. He arrived at a door at the end of the corridor and tapped three times.

'Yes?' came a student's voice from inside.

'Lomm,' whispered the teacher. 'Open up at once.'

A bolt was unfastened and the door creaked open, but only a few inches.

'Inside, quickly,' barked Mr Lomm.

The gap was just wide enough for Osbert and Isabella to squeeze into the room.

Making quite certain that the coast was clear, Mr Lomm followed his new students inside and fastened the door behind him.

Osbert glanced around the classroom. The screaming was even louder now, but strangely, it was impossible to tell where the noise was coming from. A small group of children had gathered, but they were all smiling. Osbert half-feared that they had been driven insane by Mr Lomm's legendary acts of cruelty. As the tutor walked to the front of the classroom he beckoned Osbert and Isabella towards him and reluctantly they obeyed. With every step, the sound of screaming grew louder, until they were almost deafened by the noise. Then Mr Lomm moved to one side, revealing the source of the sickening noise. There, on a desk, was a gramophone with a large brass horn and a disc spinning rapidly on the turntable.

'A devious little stratagem to mislead the Principal,' said Mr Lomm with a smile. His voice no longer grated; there was no trace of malevolence in his eyes.

'Welcome to my class,' he continued. He wound the handle of the gramophone, lifting the needle and repositioning it at the beginning of the record, so the screaming continued as before. Quickly, Mr Lomm led his new students to a corner of the room, as far from the gramophone as was possible. 'I would like to introduce Isabella Myop and Osbert Brinkhoff.'

Osbert and Isabella smiled nervously.

'And, Osbert and Isabella, let me introduce your

new classmates. Ludwig and Louis, Friedrich and Milo, and Little Olena. A Latin greeting, I think.'

'*Ave!*' they cried, and Mr Lomm nodded his head in approval.

It was a small class, but as the Principal was quite convinced that Mr Lomm was a sadistic monster, the most intelligent children were trusted to his care, in the certain hope that he would break their spirits. In fact, Mr Lomm was a kind and patient man, who had retained his position at The Institute by hiding behind a veneer of malevolence. Only his students knew the truth of the matter. Mr Lomm could tell stories like no other teacher, acting out the parts of each character, standing on his chair and jumping from desk to desk as he related the dark tales of Schwartzgarten's long and bloody past. He demanded that his students only wrote in pencil and never used their inkwells, which he could then fill with milk or peppermint cordial as he passed a large slab of chocolate around the class.

Apart from the Principal, Mr Lomm was the only teacher to live at The Institute and this was entirely due to poverty. He had been given a basement room, far below the classrooms. It was a miserable place. Water seeped through the plaster and streaked the walls in grey rivulets; the air was thick with fungus spores. The only light in the room came from a tiny window, high up in the wall. But Mr Lomm was an enterprising man, and had attempted to alleviate the gloom by pinning a coloured print of Lake Brammerhaus to the back of the door, so that he could sit on his creaky bed and pretend that he was staring out of the window. But by night, the illusion of a lakeside vista disappeared from sight. The room was nothing more than a cold cell, where moonlight seldom penetrated. Cockroaches surged across the floor and rats gnawed at the furniture, leaving droppings in Mr Lomm's shoes which he had to empty out every morning.

It was an unwholesome place to live and Mr Lomm was seldom well. The dampness of his room contributed to his bronchial condition, and his nose often dripped with glassy pearls of mucus, which he wiped away with a large pocket-handkerchief.

Mr Lomm did everything he could to protect

his students, but even he could not stand in the way of ritual. At twelve noon his students joined The Institute's other pupils for lunch in the gymnasium, no longer under the protection of their beloved tutor.

Osbert and Isabella waited in line as the housekeeper slopped out ladlefuls of grey and steaming fish goulash. Osbert took in the scene around him. There were no more than a hundred students in The Institute, and it seemed that the older they grew, the more they came to resemble their tutors. Their faces turned greyer, the sparkle extinguished in their eyes.

The tutors themselves sat at a table on the stage, far away from the stomach-churning smell of fish goulash. The Principal sat the head of the table, sipping beetroot soup noisily from his bowl. Beside him sat Doctor Zilbergeld, greedily demolishing a heaped pile of caramel cream pastries. Beside Doctor Zilbergeld sat Anatole Strauss, admiring his reflection in the back of a spoon, and beside him, Professor Ingelbrod, munching on dry cracker biscuits. Finally, beside Professor Ingelbrod, sat the hunched and miserable figure of Mr Lomm. He could not eat a morsel of food, not while his students suffered at their bowls of grey fish goulash.

'I have no appetite,' explained Mr Lomm to the Principal. 'The revolting sight of children eating turns my stomach.'

The Principal nodded in agreement.

The room was unnaturally, deathly quiet. Osbert took his seat and stared unhappily into his bowl of goulash. A fish head bobbed on the surface, staring up at Osbert through milky eyes. Wherever he went in The Institute he was being watched.

'There's something strange about his eye,' murmured Isabella.

Osbert stared quizzically at his friend.

'Not the fish head,' said Isabella. 'That man.'

A small tutor was patrolling the gymnasium, swiping at any student brave or foolish enough to raise their voice above a whisper.

'It's Mr Rudulfus,' whispered Friedrich. 'The Deputy Principal. He was blinded in a solar eclipse. He can only see through his left eye.'

As well as holding the titles of Deputy Principal and Master of Admissions, Mr Rudulfus was also head of Cosmology and Biological Science at The Institute. He had the unpleasant ability to make the universe seem vast and cold and dead. The ceiling of his schoolroom was painted a deep blue, with a detailed celestial map charting the movement of the planets. Curiously, Mr Rudulfus had demanded that the sun should be depicted orbiting around the earth. He could not accept that the earth was not at the very centre of the universe.

'Some people say you can see through the iris of his right eye and into his dark soul,' murmured Little Olena. 'But they're probably making it up.'

'They're probably not,' said Isabella gloomily.

A tall girl took the seat beside Isabella. Her face was almost cracked in two by a broad smile, which seemed peculiar and out of place among the other grim-looking students. There was no food on the girl's tray, only a glass of water and a straw.

'Hello,' whispered Isabella. 'My name is Isabella Myop.'

The girl turned to Isabella but did not utter a word. Although she still smiled, tears streamed from her eyes.

'She can't answer you,' said Little Olena.

'It's the Rudulfus Grin,' explained Friedrich. 'Mr Rudulfus has glued her mouth shut. He does that when students talk in class. He calls it Grin Gum.'

'Her name is Isidora,' said Little Olena.

The tall girl nodded and attempted to sip water through the straw, which she had managed to wiggle into position at the very corner of her mouth where the glue was weakest.

'I'm sorry,' said Isabella. 'He must be a very cruel teacher.'

'I'm sorry,' said a voice, perfectly imitating Isabella. 'He must be a very cruel teacher.'

Isabella turned suddenly. Behind her stood Mr Rudulfus, no taller than Isabella herself.

'No talking,' he hissed. 'Unless you want to end up like poor, unfortunate Isidora.' He gave a wicked grin and copied Isidora's voice, standing beside her like a ventriloquist. 'Please don't glue my mouth together, Mr Rudulfus. I promise you I won't speak another word.' He laughed and walked away.

Isabella lowered her head and silently took a mouthful of the revolting fish goulash.

———•—•———

Even at night, as lessons finished for the day and the students returned to their families, they could not entirely escape from their teachers. Many citizens in the city lived in houses and apartments that were owned by The Institute, and Anatole Strauss, the mathematics tutor, would arrive to collect the rent.

The Principal, meanwhile, would be driven by the Porter through the streets of Schwartzgarten, making quite certain that his students were locked up securely in their homes. Nobody ever discussed the cruelty of The Institute's tutors; it was safest not to. But even so, everyone knew the stories. Even the Governor of Schwartzgarten himself ruled over the city only with the blessing of The Institute. Nobody had more power than the Principal.

Mr and Mrs Brinkhoff and Nanny were waiting expectantly as Osbert returned home from The Institute.

'How was your first day, Osbert?' asked Mrs Brinkhoff anxiously.

'Very interesting,' replied Osbert, who did not want to alarm his mother.

'What did I say?' smiled Mr Brinkhoff, taking his wife's hand. 'I told you not to believe the terrible stories.'

Osbert gave Nanny a watery smile as she poured him a cup of cocoa. But Nanny was not to be fooled; she could see into his heart, and knew that all was not well.

———

Mr Lomm saw the best in all his students, but he could tell from the very first day of teaching Osbert and Isabella that they had a unique and incredible talent. They both had a good ear for music, and had been enrolled by Mr Lomm at the Academy of the fearsome Professor Ingelbrod (who also taught music at The Institute) to learn the violin.

Every year, the most gifted students of the Academy had the opportunity to sit the examination for the Constantin Violin. The instrument had been a gift to The Institute, presented by the first Governor of Schwartzgarten seventy years before. It had been crafted by the master violin-maker Constantin Esterburg, who had also served as court musician to Good Prince Eugene, who had ruled over Schwartzgarten many decades before. After sitting the written paper, any student fortunate enough to attain a score of over ninety per cent would then be presented with the Constantin Violin for an entire year. There had been no successful candidates in over sixty years, and no one was happier about this than the Principal.

One afternoon, as Mr Lomm dismissed his students for the day, he invited Osbert and Isabella for cocoa in his basement room. As he led them across the courtyard, he was suddenly arrested by a sharp voice from above.

'What are you doing, Lomm?' cried the Principal, leaning from his window in the great tower above The Institute.

'Punishment,' barked Mr Lomm.

'Very good,' replied the Principal, glowering at Osbert. 'Continue.' He closed his window, and Osbert and Isabella followed Mr Lomm as he descended the narrow stone steps to his basement room.

Osbert was always impressed by the speed with which Mr Lomm could transform from a kind and understanding teacher to assume the role of the Principal's vile and vindictive protégé. Mr Lomm opened the door to his room and led Osbert and Isabella inside.

As the cocoa simmered in a pan, Mr Lomm opened the cupboard on the wall, spluttering and waving his arms in the air as a cloud of grey moths flew from inside. He gave a sigh and removed a scuffed and faded blue case.

'I wanted to show you this,' said Mr Lomm, unfastening the case and removing an elegant, yet battered, violin. 'Not quite the Constantin Violin, but the first instrument I ever played.' He held the violin to his chin. Drawing the bow across the strings he played a single note; a beautiful note that seemed to fill the room. He smiled and took two ancient and identical books from a shelf and presented them to Osbert and Isabella.

Osbert turned the dusty pages of the leather-bound volume: *The Virtue of the Violin* by Constantin Esterburg.

'In six weeks,' continued Mr Lomm, 'The Institute will hold the examination for the Constantin Violin. It is an instrument with a tragic history. On the very night that Constantin Esterburg finished composing his first opera, he was thrown from his carriage and into the surging waters of the River Schwartz. Alas, the poor man might have been saved, had he not tried to rescue his precious violin. His body was discovered three weeks later, miraculously still dressed in his court finery and powdered wig. His eyes had been pecked out by wading birds, and his legs had been eaten as far as the kneecaps by blue trout. But in his grey, withered hands, Constantin still clutched the violin to his chest.'

Osbert and Isabella were almost breathless as they listened to Mr Lomm recounting the tale.

'As you know, the violin has never been awarded to a student in living memory. I think the two of you have the ability to change this.'

Osbert's heart beat hard against his chest. Could

such a thing be possible? Might he one day hold a violin to his chin that had been pulled from the skeletal hands of the great Constantin Esterberg? He was certain his heart would explode with excitement.

CHAPTER FOUR

A S LESSONS finished for the day, Professor Ingelbrod would lead his students out of The Institute and down the hill to his Academy of Music.

There was something peculiar about the way the Professor walked, almost as though he was a tinplate figure, wound by a key, like the toys Osbert had played with as a small boy. Professor Ingelbrod suffered from a hunched spine, due in part to a lifetime of bending over to hit his students. To correct this disfigurement, he would lace himself into a rigid leather corset, which supported his spine but prevented any movement from his chest to his waist. This contributed to his poisonous temper and outbursts of violence.

The Academy stood in a quiet street, where the screams of the Professor's tutees could not be heard. It was a tall, rectangular building, which stretched like a tombstone into the grey skies shrouding the city of Schwartzgarten.

And every evening, between the hours of five o'clock and seven o'clock, the students would practise the violin, under Professor Ingelbrod's hawk-like eye.

As a young man, the Professor had studied the violin at the conservatoire in the city of Lüchmünster, where he dreamt of playing first violin in the city's celebrated orchestra. But his dreams were not matched by his talents. As he drew his bow over the catgut strings, it was as though the unfortunate cat had come back to life, mewing and shrieking with every stroke.

It was a bitter evening in the Academy, and Osbert's fingers trembled in the icy music room as he clipped the shoulder rest to the underside of his violin. His father had given him the instrument, which he himself had used as a boy.

'Don't stoop, Slack-spine!' barked Professor Ingelbrod. 'It'll be the worse for you if you do.'

It was not an idle threat; Professor Ingelbrod was a cruel and sadistic violin teacher. He kept two heavy iron frames in the corner of the music room, to teach his 'slack-spined' students to stand upright while playing the violin. He would screw the clamps to their hands and legs, fixing them securely in position. From the arms of the antiquated contraption sprouted a long iron rod, attached to which was yet another metal clamp. This clamp was the most uncomfortable of all, and was used to immobilise the neck and head of Professor Ingelbrod's tutees. Friedrich in particular had spent many long hours in the corner of the room, his arms, legs and head screwed into the agonisingly uncomfortable iron frame. Bertold, an older boy from The Institute, had developed a hunched back from his time inside the frame.

'Now *play*, boy,' demanded Professor Ingelbrod.

Osbert remembered everything he had read in Mr Lomm's book. He stood bolt upright with his chest puffed out, his shoulders pulled back, the violin resting on his left shoulder. The bow was carefully balanced between Osbert's thumb and fingers as it slid smoothly over the strings.

'Enough, enough!' snarled Professor Ingelbrod rising from his desk, violin bow in hand. He held his hands to his ears as if in excruciating pain. 'I'd rather listen to a dying dog in the gutter.'

Osbert's playing was exemplary, but to make this admission to the child would, he felt sure, be seen as a sign of weakness.

'And next? Who will play *next?*'

He walked slowly through the music room, observing his students with an icy gaze. At length, his glance fell on Isabella, who sat shivering at the back of the room.

'You,' whispered the Professor, and tapped Isabella twice on the shoulder with his violin bow. Isabella sighed quietly and stood up, taking her violin with her to the front of the class.

'Well?' rasped the Professor. 'What are you waiting for?'

Isabella began to play. It was a mournful composition, written by Professor Ingelbrod himself and entitled, 'Death Stalks Us Through The Shadows'.

The Professor rapped the desk sharply with his violin bow. 'Enough,' he cried, stalking towards Isabella, who flinched in fear.

Professor Ingelbrod advanced on the girl, every joint in his body cracking, as though his bones were splintering under the skin. He seized her by the arm and dragged her to the corner of the room.

'The iron frame,' he hissed, unscrewing the metal bolts and freeing Friedrich, who was so exhausted he almost fell to the floor as his limbs were released. 'Step over here,' said the Professor smiling, and beckoning Isabella towards the iron embrace of his instrument of torture. 'Only then can you stand a chance of improving as a musician.'

But again, Professor Ingelbrod was not telling the truth. Isabella was one of the most gifted violinists he had ever heard. His own talent was pitiful in comparison; the harder he tried, the more discordant and grotesque the noise became. As Ingelbrod screwed Isabella's arms and neck into position in the metal stand, he drew hollow consolation from the look of terror in poor Isabella's eyes.

———

Fate seemed to be smiling on Osbert when the Myop family, who were bakers, bought the deserted pastry shop across the street from the Brinkhoff apartment. It was a happy place to spend time. Osbert's heart would skip as he sat with Isabella, watching as she sipped from her enormous cup of spiced hot chocolate, wiping the moustache of whipped cream from her upper lip. Osbert loved the smell of fresh baking; he loved to help Mrs Myop as she stocked the shop window with honey cakes and pretzels. He would stand for hours and watch Mr Myop as he baked plaits of dark rye bread.

One cold morning, Osbert entered the pastry shop and peered over the counter. Mrs Myop, who had dreams of singing at the Schwartzgarten Opera House, trilled noisily as she piled custard pastries on a tray, her soprano voice cutting through the air like knife blades.

'Good morning, Mrs Myop,' said Osbert. 'I've come for Isabella.'

Mrs Myop stopped singing, mid-aria. 'Osbert Brinkhoff!' said the woman, delighted. She bellowed upstairs. 'Isabella. Darling angel. Osbert Brinkhoff has come to walk you to school.' Her voice was so loud that the trays of pastries rattled on the counter and the glass of the shop window seemed to tremble.

Osbert walked with Isabella to the tram stop and

they journeyed up to The Institute together, with pastries in hand to fortify them on their way.

'Do you think the Principal is a *very* old man?' asked Isabella, brushing crumbs from her overcoat.

'He wasn't even young when my father was a boy,' said Osbert.

'Some people get too old,' continued Isabella, engrossed in thought. 'It's very important to know *when* to die.'

Osbert stared hard at his friend and they continued walking in silence.

Mr Lomm had been badly affected by the coldness of the day. His throat was wrapped tightly in a woollen scarf, and he dabbed constantly at his dribbling nostrils with a grey pocket handkerchief. But Mr Lomm was undaunted, his eyes burned with the unmistakable glow of hope. He wound the handle of the gramophone and turned the brass horn towards the door; the wailing of children continued as before.

'It is sometimes possible to listen to a piece of music for the very first time,' said Mr Lomm as his students feasted on nougat and peppermint cordial, 'and tell for a fact how a passage will end. If the notes will go up, or if the notes will go down. As with mathematics, often there are inevitable musical outcomes.'

Osbert smiled. In his mind there was one inevitable outcome to life; that Isabella would remain at his side forever.

Outside Mr Lomm's classroom the Porter lurked in the shadows, his ear pressed hard against the door. Something was not right; the screams of Mr Lomm's students seemed louder than ever, and he was determined to find out why.

———

Each and every afternoon Mr Lomm would wheel the gramophone to the door of his classroom, where the spinning record of screaming children would drown out the beautiful violin music of his protégés, Osbert and Isabella.

Mr Lomm's book recommended at least fifteen minutes of violin practice at home each day, but Osbert always played for longer, gazing across the street towards the apartment of the Myop family. And every evening

Isabella would appear at the window and blow a single kiss to Osbert, before pulling the shutters closed for the night.

'Isabella,' whispered Osbert. 'Beautiful Isabella.'

Three weeks before the examination for the Constantin Violin, the instrument was removed from the bank vaults of Muller, Baum and Spink and put on display in a glass cabinet in The Institute's gymnasium, resting on a cushion of purple velvet. The neck of the violin was carved from a block of maple, finished at the end with a beautiful ornamental scroll. The back of the violin was made of fiddleback maple and the front of spruce from the great forest beyond Schwartzgarten, edged with an inlay of ebonised pear wood. The grain was as bright as orange flame against the amber-coloured wood. A painting hung above the cabinet, a portrait of Constantin in his powdered wig, clutching the violin in his long and elegant fingers. The students of The Institute crowded around the cabinet.

'They say one of Constantin's eyeballs was discovered inside the violin,' said Louis.

'I heard one of his leg bones was made into the bow,' said Ludwig.

The stories were macabre and plentiful, but it was still the most beautiful instrument Osbert had ever set eyes upon. Every day he would stand in the gymnasium, gazing into the cabinet at the unrivalled violin.

———

Although all of Mr Lomm's students were exceptional, he decided that only Osbert and Isabella should be recommended to sit the examination for the Constantin Violin; he felt sure that they would not be broken by the cruel and merciless rigours of the exam process.

Every year the teachers of The Institute would compile questions for the exam paper; so fiendishly difficult were they that the candidates stood little chance of answering even one question correctly.

Every night, Osbert would carry home huge armfuls of books, poring over them for hours at a time by the light of his father's desk lamp.

'He's got thin,' whispered Nanny as Mr Brinkhoff lifted his son from the study chair and carried him upstairs to bed.

'*Amo, ama*s, *amat*,' murmured Osbert, reciting Latin in his sleep. '*Amamus, amatis, amant...*'

'It's not good for a boy to learn so much,' continued Nanny, following Mr Brinkhoff up the stairs. 'It's not natural. And he gets no fresh air. His eyes will dry up with so much reading, and drop from their sockets. And then where will he be? That's what I ask you.'

'The job worth starting is worth finishing,' replied Mrs Brinkhoff, but she had also grown concerned. Osbert had always been a serious boy, but in the weeks leading up to the examination he had become quieter, his skin had grown paler, his expression more sombre. She wished bitterly that Osbert had been born a slow and stupid boy and that he had never been accepted into The Institute in the first place. After all, many slow and stupid people went to work in banks, and she still harboured her furtive dream of the bank of Brinkhoff and Brinkhoff.

The day of the examination dawned. It was a thick, grey morning, almost indistinguishable from night. Osbert took a pocket torch as he walked with Isabella to the tram terminus.

'What is the rule of Pythagoras?' asked Isabella as the tram emerged through the shroud of fog.

'The square on the hypotenuse is equal to the sum of the squares on the other two sides,' replied Osbert.

'Correct,' said Isabella, climbing on board with her friend as the bell sounded and the tram rattled on along the south bank of the River Schwartz, slicing cleanly through the enveloping fog. There was something supernatural about the weather, as though the Principal was somehow capable of making the morning even more unpleasant than it needed to be.

Osbert and Isabella pulled books from their satchels and began to read, extracting every last ounce of knowledge the volumes had to give.

'What is pi?' asked Osbert as they entered the gates of The Institute and crossed the courtyard together.

'Pie is delicious,' replied Isabella, smiling. Osbert smiled back.

They entered the great, grey building and hurried along the corridors, past the hall clock and the hissing gas lamps. Osbert could remember how disorientating it had once been to negotiate the maze of passageways. Now he was convinced he could walk to the gymnasium with his eyes closed.

They opened the door to the vast and echoing room. The older students of The Institute, selected by their respective teachers in the certain knowledge that they would fail miserably, already sat at their desks, greyer than ever and dead of eye.

'You're late,' grunted Mr Lomm, who stood in front of the stage, grasping the examination papers in his hands. His words were sharp but his eyes still sparkled. He did not dare to smile.

The curtains on the stage twitched; as usual, they were being watched.

Mr Lomm placed the exam papers on the desks as Osbert and Isabella took their seats.

'You have three hours,' said Mr Lomm. 'No more.' Then, whispering so he could not be overheard, he added, 'I *know* you can do it.'

He glanced up at the clock on the wall. 'You may begin.'

Osbert and Isabella picked up their pens and slowly, methodically, filled in their exam papers.

———◆———

A teaching position at The Institute carried with it many privileges, and not only the ill-treatment of children. Each and every tutor was entitled to membership of the notorious Offenbach Club. For Mr Lomm it was an odious honour and one that he found particularly disagreeable. Unfortunately for him, membership was compulsory.

The secret society had been established by the late Julius Offenbach only a month before his untimely end in the boiling bathtub. The club met every second Tuesday of the month in a private room above the Old Chop House in the very heart of Schwartzgarten. Mr Lomm hated attending the monthly meetings. The Old Chop House was a dismal place; even his mouldering basement room at The Institute seemed pleasant by comparison.

Struggling through the crowded public bar,

which reeked of rye beer and cigar smoke, Mr Lomm climbed the stairs to the private dining room of the Offenbach Club. A smile flickered across his lips – something was lifting his spirits. In his hands he clutched the exam papers.

He knocked once at the door and entered the dining room. The walls were panelled with dark oak, and the low-beamed ceiling made the room even darker and more claustrophobic. The long table, which dominated the room, was set for dinner. The other teachers of The Institute had already taken their places. A particularly gloomy piece of music played through the enormous brass horn of the gramophone in the corner of the room, wound at intervals by the Porter.

'You're late,' said the Principal, as Mr Lomm sat down.

'I do apologise,' whispered Mr Lomm. 'I've been correlating the examination results. It took a little longer than I expected.'

The waiter was serving medallions of veal in a thick red wine sauce. He was an elderly man, hunched at the shoulders. He was both deaf and mute, deliberately picked so as never to report on the secret meetings of the Offenbach Club.

'Well,' asked the Principal, chewing noisily on a mouthful of veal. 'What were the scores?'

It was a struggle for Mr Lomm to retain his composure. He wanted to climb to his feet and scream the examination results at the top of his voice.

'We're waiting,' growled the Principal.

The waiter slopped a slice of veal onto Mr Lomm's plate, splashing the teacher's neatly pressed shirt with the dark red sauce.

Mr Lomm hesitated. 'The Myop girl scored ninety-two per cent…'

Mr Rudulfus gulped. 'And the Brinkhoff boy?'

It was becoming increasingly difficult for Mr Lomm to contain his excitement.

'Failed, did he?' barked Doctor Zilbergeld.

'Not exactly,' replied Lomm.

'Well?' insisted the Principal.

The teachers waited expectantly.

'Osbert Brinkhoff achieved a perfect score.'

'What?' roared the Principal.

'A perfect score,' repeated Mr Lomm.

'I heard what you said,' spluttered the Principal, spraying the white tablecloth with a fine mist of red wine sauce.

'How could this have happened?' demanded Anatole Strauss.

'Perhaps the little swine cheated?' suggested Doctor Zilbergeld, her voice drilling into Mr Lomm's already aching head.

'Impossible,' he replied. 'The exam papers were kept under lock and key by the Principal himself.'

'What are we going to *do*?' demanded Mr Rudulfus. What little colour he had in his face had drained away, leaving him ashen.

'There's nothing we can do,' said Mr Lomm carefully. His heart beat rapidly in his throat. Osbert had beaten The Institute; the violin was his. 'I suppose we must give the wretched Brinkhoff boy the Constantin Violin.'

'We shall do no such thing, Mr Lomm,' said the Principal, folding his napkin and mopping the traces of gravy from the corners of his mouth.

'I beg your pardon?' croaked Mr Lomm. His heart was beating so fast, he was certain it would rip a hole in his chest and burst through his suit onto the crisp white tablecloth.

'We must crush Osbert Brinkhoff,' continued the Principal. 'To award the boy the violin would be to admit defeat. And so it must remain under lock and key.'

There were murmurs of agreement from around the table. 'Then the matter is settled. It is the opinion of us all.'

Mr Lomm coughed anxiously. He could not be party to such a despicable arrangement. 'It is not the opinion of *all* of us,' he stammered.

The Principal gasped and craned his long neck forward, observing Lomm closely.

'You don't think we might be *wrong* to do this?' whispered Mr Lomm.

'Wrong?' The Principal's tone was so deep and ominous that the table seemed to vibrate, the glasses rattling.

'But surely,' said Mr Rudulfus, certain that the

Principal was about to erupt in a volcanic fit of rage, 'surely you understand better than any of us the need to suppress such insolent intelligence. You, who have broken the spirits of so many students with your cruelty.'

'I don't understand,' growled the Principal. 'Why are you attempting to defend the boy?'

'I think I can explain, sir,' came a voice.

The Porter, who had been biding his time in the shadows, rose from his chair and approached the table. In his hands he held a smooth black disc.

'Well?' said the Principal impatiently. 'Speak.'

'I think this can speak for me,' replied the Porter, placing the disc on the gramophone in the corner of the room and winding the handle. He positioned the needle on the spinning record, which hissed and crackled. Suddenly, an ear-splitting scream echoed from the horn of the machine.

'Where did you get this?' demanded the Principal.

'Took it from his room,' grinned the Porter, jabbing his thumb in the direction of Mr Lomm. 'Knew something wasn't right. Don't get screams like that without a death or two along the way. Said to myself, "This doesn't add up." And it didn't, did it?'

'We thought you were the cruellest teacher of us all,' stammered Anatole Strauss.

'You lied to us?' screeched Doctor Zilbergeld, lifting the needle from the gramophone.

'You traitor!' screamed Professor Ingelbrod. 'Slackspine!'

He snatched the gramophone record from Doctor Zilbergeld, flinging it across the dinner table with such speed and force that it narrowly avoided slicing off the top of Mr Lomm's neatly oiled head, like the top of a roasted egg.

Mr Lomm was trapped. His secret had been discovered. 'Yes, I lied!' he began, stumbling over his words. 'I've been protecting the children from you. I tell them stories. I give them peppermint cordial and chocolate. I want them to be happy.' There was another gasp from the tutors. 'Yes,' he repeated, '*happy*! It's bad enough that you make the children's lives a misery. But to deprive Osbert of a prize which is rightfully his? It's wrong. Terribly wrong.'

Defiantly he rose from the table, although his knees were buckling from the strain. 'I don't want any part of it.'

'Get out,' said the Principal icily, his face white with fury. '*Get out!*'

Still grinning, the Porter opened the door.

Banished from the room, Lomm returned home to The Institute as the meeting of the Offenbach Club continued.

An agreement was passed around the table, attesting to the fact that Osbert should not be presented with the violin.

'Lomm has failed us,' said the Principal. 'I trust you will all make the correct decision and together we shall crush the Brinkhoff boy.'

Each of the teachers, in turn, signed their names in red ink.

The next morning, Mr Lomm was summoned to the Principal's office. He was so nervous that he could feel a tingling sensation down his left arm and feared that he was suffering a heart attack.

The Principal observed Mr Lomm silently, enjoying every delicious moment of suspense.

'So,' he began at last, 'you thought you could betray me, did you? Betray the Offenbach Club and everything The Institute stands for?'

'But Osbert Brinkhoff achieved a perfect score in his examination,' stammered Mr Lomm. 'It is only right that he should be presented with the Constantin Violin.'

'Right?' spat the Principal. '*Right?* I thought you were different, Lomm. I thought you were exceptional. A tutor to strike fear into the very hearts of the students. A man to carry on the legacy of The Institute. That is what I thought, but clearly I was mistaken. You will never work in Schwartzgarten again.' He turned his back and glared out of the window. The interview was at an end.

'I'll leave this afternoon,' said Mr Lomm.

Pulling the door shut behind him, he returned to his dank basement room and packed his clothes and books into a single suitcase.

Osbert and Isabella watched in disbelief from the window of the gymnasium as Mr Lomm stepped from the school building and into the courtyard. In one hand he carried his battered leather suitcase and in the other his ancient violin case. Mr Lomm turned awkwardly and smiled up at Osbert and Isabella. But no sooner had the smile formed on his lips, than he became aware of a sharp tapping noise high above him. It was the Principal, beating on his window with the silver tip of his walking cane.

The Porter scuttled from his room and unlocked the great wrought-iron gates.

'And good riddance to you,' he grinned. 'You're no better than a treacherous gutter rat.'

Mr Lomm stepped through the open gateway and was gone.

Chapter Five

THE INSTITUTE had been founded during the reign of Good Prince Eugene, an excellent swordsman who decreed that as long as The Institute remained standing, the students should be taught the noble sport of fencing.

The Principal was a man of unwavering tradition, and saw to it that Prince Eugene's edict was followed to the letter. The day after Lomm's departure, the students of The Institute gathered in the gymnasium, dressed in white fencing jackets and breeches. Osbert glanced anxiously around the room. Something was wrong. The Principal had also summoned the tutors to the gymnasium, where they sat in a row with barely suppressed smirks of amusement.

As an eerie silence fell, the Principal entered the great hall. He carried with him his own golden rapier, which had once belonged to Prince Eugene himself, the tip of the blade monogrammed with the initials of its illustrious former owner. The Principal's love of fencing was twofold: he enjoyed the art and history of fencing, but even more than that, he enjoyed the opportunity of injuring his students in the name of sport.

There was a palpable sense of anticipation in the gymnasium and the Principal relished every last second of it. He smiled. The students were awaiting the results of the examination for the Constantin Violin.

'We have to find out,' whispered Isabella, her impatience finally getting the better of her.

'Who is it? Who's talking?' barked the Principal.

There was silence in the room. Slowly, Osbert stepped forward.

'Well?' asked the Principal at last. 'What is it? Speak up.'

Osbert held his fencing rapier tightly in his hand. 'Excuse me, sir?' he said, his voice quavering.

'Yes?' said the Principal, a thin smile forming on his blue lips.

'The Constantin Violin, sir…' said Osbert weakly.

'You want to know if you've been awarded the violin?' continued the Principal, archly.

Osbert nodded.

'Perhaps we should continue this conversation on the piste,' said the Principal, taking his position on the raised platform in the centre of the room. Osbert stepped up; he was preparing to make the salute when the Principal lunged with his sword. Osbert retreated, almost losing his footing.

'So,' hissed the Principal, 'you thought you were clever enough to pass the examination, did you?'

Osbert parried, deflecting the Principal's rapier.

'Good,' said the Principal. 'Very good. If only your exam paper had been as good as your fencing.'

Osbert could not understand. He was certain that he had passed the examination.

The Principal watched narrowly, smiling all the time. 'Yet again, we are unable to award the Constantin Violin to a student of The Institute. And so the instrument will remain in the bank vaults of Muller, Baum and Spink for another year.'

'But that isn't fair,' said Osbert.

'Life, as you well know, is not fair,' snapped the Principal.

In a sudden fit of rage, Osbert lunged forward with his rapier.

'*Glissard!*' shouted the Principal, deflecting the lunge and knocking the rapier from Osbert's hand. 'Dare to question me, will you?'

Osbert staggered backwards as the Principal advanced menacingly.

The Principal's words were sharper than any rapier blow, and seemed to force Osbert to the ground. The Principal held the tip of his rapier to the boy's nose. With a lightning movement, he cut at Osbert's face. The boy cried out, as much in surprise as in pain.

The Principal stepped back.

Osbert held his hand to his cheek; his fingers were red and sticky.

'First blood,' whispered the Principal. 'You are expelled, boy!' An expression of grim satisfaction spread across his face. 'I'll bring your pitiable family to their knees, you mark my words, Osbert Brinkhoff.'

'You didn't question the Principal?' asked Mrs Brinkhoff, her voice trembling as she spoke.

Osbert simply nodded. The blood had dried to a crusty scab on his face, but it would take longer to heal the deeper wounds that had opened that afternoon. As Mrs Brinkhoff dabbed at the rapier cut with a cotton wool ball dipped in antiseptic lotion, she feared that life was about to change forever.

The following morning at eight o'clock, as Mr Baum crossed the chequered floor of the banking hall and unbolted the front door, he was surprised to find a customer already standing outside, shrouded in mist.

'Good morning, sir,' said the banker. 'I trust I haven't kept you?'

The figure stepped forward, clutching a silver-topped Malacca cane in his grey, bony hand. Mr Baum recoiled in horror; it was the skeletal frame of the Principal.

'It's a minute past eight,' hissed the Principal. 'You have kept me waiting for precisely sixty seconds.'

'I do apologise,' whispered Mr Baum, half bowing.

'I wish to speak to Mr Spink,' said the Principal, removing his hat and entering the bank. 'On a matter of grave importance.'

'I shall telephone him at once,' replied Mr Baum.

'No time, no time!' snapped the Principal, crossing the banking hall and climbing into the elevator. Before Mr Baum could say another word, the Principal pulled the gate shut behind him and pushed the button for the second floor.

Mr Spink, who was well-stricken in years and particularly susceptible to shock, was similarly surprised and dismayed upon opening his door to discover the Principal standing outside. It was customary for the Principal to summon Mr Spink to The Institute when he wished to discuss business matters and he seldom ventured into the beating heart of the city.

'This is indeed an honour,' murmured Mr Spink. 'I don't believe we've seen you at the bank since old Mr Muller was still alive and breathing.'

'Enough!' barked the Principal. 'Sit.'

Mr Spink sat, obediently.

The Principal remained standing, looming over Mr Spink's desk like a deathly apparition. He lowered his voice to a menacing growl. 'It is necessary that you dismiss Mr Brinkhoff.'

'May I ask why?' inquired Mr Spink, utterly bewildered.

The Principal's eyes twitched, and Mr Spink flinched, shrinking back in his chair.

'You must make an example of the man,' demanded the Principal. 'His son dared to question The Institute, and so we expelled him. We will not tolerate insubordination. The boy's father is undoubtedly to blame. It is a known fact that insubordination begins at home.'

'But surely,' began Mr Spink hesitantly, 'a certain amount of boisterousness is only to be expected from a boy so clever?'

'Too much knowledge is a dangerous thing,' barked the Principal, banging his cane on the mahogany desk to emphasise his point. 'Do you understand?'

Mr Spink winced; every tap of the Principal's cane created yet another dent on his immaculately polished desk.

'Mr Brinkhoff has always been a good worker,' said Mr Spink, cautiously, anxious not to displease the Principal. 'Are you absolutely *sure* you want me to dismiss him?'

The Principal leant forward, resting his bony fingers on the edge of Mr Spink's desk and glowered at the bank manager. 'You know what will happen if you don't.'

<hr>

Mr Brinkhoff sat in his small office, which overlooked the park and the mountains beyond. It was a dark morning, and he worked by the light of his desk lamp. The room was cluttered with pens and bottles of ink, date stamps and blotters. He took a sip of black tea and replaced the cup on the saucer. Looking out of the window, he noticed a familiar figure standing in the street below. It was the Principal. As if aware that he was being observed, he turned and looked up. He raised his hat and smiled at Mr Brinkhoff, before turning and walking quickly away from the bank.

The telephone rang noisily, rattling the teacup and saucer. Mr Brinkhoff answered.

'Good morning, Muller, Baum and Spink. Brinkhoff speaking.'

'Brinkhoff, this is Spink.' The man was anxious and the words caught in his throat. 'Would you come to my office, please?'

Gripped by a sudden sense of foreboding, Mr Brinkhoff hurried along the passageway to Mr Spink's office and knocked timidly at the door.

'Come,' said Mr Spink.

'Good morning, Mr Spink, sir,' said Mr Brinkhoff, anticipating the worst.

'Take a seat,' said Mr Spink, and Mr Brinkhoff sat, awkwardly. 'It has been brought to my attention, Brinkhoff…' began Mr Spink. He hesitated. He had no idea how to continue his sentence. He knew he had to sack Mr Brinkhoff, but he could find no convincing reason for doing so. Mr Brinkhoff was polite, hard-working, well-mannered, punctual, kind, generous, loyal; in every respect he was a model employee.

Mr Brinkhoff watched as his employer dabbed at the corner of his eye with a pocket handkerchief. 'You're going to sack me, aren't you?' he inquired quietly.

Mr Spink sighed, sadly. 'The Principal expressly wishes it. Put yourself in my position. What would you do? We cannot enrage The Institute. Just think how much money they have in our vaults, Brinkhoff. If they closed their account it would be a catastrophe. The Bank of Muller, Baum and Spink would be destroyed.'

'But I haven't done anything *wrong*,' pleaded Mr Brinkhoff.

Mr Spink moaned. He was not a heroic man. There was nothing he would have liked more than to keep Mr Brinkhoff in the offices of Muller, Baum and Spink, but that was not to be. The Institute had spoken.

———

Day after day Mr Brinkhoff lay in bed, or sat silently in his study. He was a broken man. As Osbert had been expelled from The Institute, Mrs Brinkhoff had no choice but to continue the boy's education at home, and this she did every morning. Then every afternoon she would make nourishing soups and broths, which she fed to Mr Brinkhoff, holding his hand gently and hoping for the best. Nanny, fearing the dark times ahead, would sit alone in her bedroom with a bottle of plum brandy, puffing at a fat cigar and staring grimly at the photographs of her dead, lost loves. Left to his own devices, Osbert would spend his afternoons in the cemetery, wandering the avenues and reading the inscriptions on the gravestones and elaborate marble tombs. He felt that he was to blame for his father's dismissal and the deathly calm of the cemetery soothed his troubled mind.

All the time the Brinkhoffs' finances dwindled until, one evening, three weeks after Mr Brinkhoff's departure from the offices of Muller, Baum and Spink, there came a loud rap at the front door of their apartment. Nanny had gone to the bar at the corner of the street for a 'glug of something medicinal', so Osbert answered the door instead. There, on the landing, stood Anatole Strauss. He was a fat and ugly man, with greasy black hair and a rigidly waxed moustache.

'Good evening, Mr Strauss,' said Osbert politely.

'I'm here to see your parents,' said Strauss, his moustache quivering. 'It's about the rent they owe The Institute. They're two weeks in arrears.'

Not waiting to be invited inside, Anatole Strauss strode through the door and into the sitting room, where Mr Brinkhoff sat in an armchair, wrapped in a blanket. Mrs Brinkhoff appeared from the kitchen, carrying a tray of apple dumplings and a pot of steaming hot coffee.

'I see,' said Strauss, rubbing his hands triumphantly. 'You don't have enough money to pay your rent to The Institute, but you *do* have enough to fritter away on apple dumplings and coffee.'

'But my father is ill,' said Osbert.

'And we have to eat,' added Mrs Brinkhoff quietly.

'Maybe you do and maybe you don't,' snapped Anatole Strauss. 'That isn't the point and well you know it.' He glanced in the mirror, tightening the tips of his moustache. 'Imagine,' he continued, 'if every one of The Institute's tenants refused to pay their rent. What then?'

'We aren't refusing to pay,' replied Mr Brinkhoff,

meekly. 'It's just that we don't have the money to pay you.'

Osbert wanted to kick Anatole Strauss very hard, but thought better of it.

'Refusing to pay, or not refusing to pay but having no money, it all adds up to the same thing,' continued Strauss. 'Or rather, it doesn't add up to anything at all. You've got three days to raise the money to clear your debts.'

'Three days?' echoed Mr Brinkhoff. 'That doesn't give us any time at all.'

'Please,' begged Mrs Brinkhoff. 'If you gave us a week?'

'I'll give you three days, and no more,' barked Anatole Strauss. 'Three days and you're out on the street!'

———◆———

That night Mr and Mrs Brinkhoff sat in their cold dining room, wrapped in overcoats and mufflers to keep themselves warm. There was no coal to feed the fire, no electric light to cheer them. By the light of a candle, Mr Brinkhoff opened the family cash tin and emptied the contents. Three small brass coins rolled out onto the table, along with a dinner token for the Emperor Xavier Hotel, long since expired.

'Is that all?' whispered Mrs Brinkhoff, greatly disappointed.

'Yes,' replied her husband, brokenly, gathering up the coins. 'Just a handful of brass curselings. We don't have a single imperial crown to our name.'

There was nothing they could do but wait.

———

Anatole Strauss was as good as his word, and on the morning of the third day he arrived to evict Mr and Mrs Brinkhoff, Osbert and Nanny from the apartment. There was a loud knock at the door, a violent tremor which seemed to shake the building to its very foundations.

'Don't answer it,' said Osbert.

'Perhaps he'll go away,' whispered Mrs Brinkhoff.

'If we don't let him in he'll return with the

police,' replied Mr Brinkhoff. 'And then what will become of us?'

Resigned to their fate, Mrs Brinkhoff unlocked the door. In the hallway outside the apartment stood two bailiffs. They bowed and raised their hats.

'Nothing personal, of course,' said the first bailiff.

'We've all got to earn a crust,' said the second bailiff.

'Enough of that,' roared Strauss. 'The Brinkhoffs have not earned our pity.' He clapped his hands and the bailiffs scurried in through the door.

The Brinkhoff family were forced downstairs onto the pavement, watching in silence as their worldly possessions were carried out into the street.

'I'm sorry,' said the first bailiff, holding out his hand and motioning to the violin that Osbert carried. Osbert was so furious he wanted to bite the bailiff, but he did not. Instead he took the instrument from its case and gazed at it for the final time. He closed the case and handed it to the bailiff.

'What's all this?' wheezed Nanny, as she heaved into sight, returning from the market with what little food she had been able to beg or borrow from the stall-holders.

'None of your concern,' replied Anatole Strauss, bristling.

'That's mine!' screeched Nanny as the second bailiff appeared from inside with a black raven-feather hat.

'And now it's The Institute's,' retorted Strauss.

Nanny fished a large and earthy beetroot from the bottom of her bag and hurled it at the bailiff's head with such force that it knocked the man from his feet and into the murky water that flowed along the gutter.

'Any more of that and I'll call for the police,' cried the first bailiff, only to be hit square between the eyes by a hard, dry lump of rye bread.

Anatole Strauss took cover behind the wagon that he had hired to transport his ill-gotten spoils. He waited out of sight until the last of the Brinkhoffs' possessions were dragged out onto the street.

Osbert looked up at the Myop apartment above the pastry shop, and saw Isabella standing at the window, her nose pressed against the glass. Life for his friend was quite unchanged. Isabella had remained a student of The Institute and still had the luxury of a roof over her head. She waved forlornly, but Osbert did not have the spirit left in him to wave back.

'And this,' said Anatole Strauss, appearing from behind the wagon with a large brass padlock which he fastened to the door of the Brinkhoffs' apartment, 'this is so you won't be tempted to get back inside!' He surveyed the heaped furniture on the street before him. 'I doubt this bric-a-brac is enough to raise the money you owe The Institute, but it's the *principle* of the matter.'

Nanny, who had been waiting patiently, heaved a can of salted pilchards at the man, knocking his Homburg hat from his head. Like an insect fleeing for safety, Anatole Strauss turned and hurried away, the bailiffs scurrying behind him, wheeling the wagon as they went.

The Brinkhoffs stood on the pavement, utterly bewildered by what had happened to them. They were left with nothing more than two old suitcases containing their second-best clothes and Mr Brinkhoff's overcoat of Brammerhaus tweed, a threadbare rug, a wicker chair that had lost its back and a stuffed parakeet, badly moth-eaten, in a glass case.

'What do we do now?' asked Mrs Brinkhoff.

'You'll have to come and live with me,' said Nanny firmly, taking charge of matters. 'I've still got my apartment in the Old Town.'

'We couldn't possibly impose,' said Mrs Brinkhoff.

'You've got no choice,' said Nanny. 'I always take care of the families I work for. Whether they can see they need the help or they can't.'

Mrs Brinkhoff smiled uncomfortably at the thought of moving to Nanny's apartment, but the family had nowhere else to go. Osbert remembered the place well, and shivered at the prospect of having to live there. He looked up again at Isabella, who smiled sadly. Mrs Myop pulled her daughter from the window and fastened the shutters.

Picking up their suitcases, the Brinkhoff family followed Nanny across the Princess Euphenia Bridge and into the Old Town.

Nanny tugged the dustsheets from the furniture and pulled cobwebs from the windows, sending a cluster of spiders scuttling into the shadows.

'How beautiful,' said Mrs Brinkhoff, her eyes straining in the dimly lit room.

But it was not a beautiful apartment. In truth, it was the most unpleasant apartment Mrs Brinkhoff had ever laid eyes on: the wallpaper was yellow with age, the paint on the doors was blistered and peeling and patches of black mould covered the ceilings. There was a tiny kitchen with a gas stove, an icebox and cold running water. There were only two bedrooms, and so Nanny generously volunteered to sleep on the battered leather sofa in the sitting room.

'You save your bones,' she insisted. 'A cobbled street's as good as a feather bed to me. And a sofa's luxury through and through. I won't lose a wink here.'

So Mr and Mrs Brinkhoff had one bedroom and Osbert had the other.

Mr Brinkhoff, who had grown weaker as the day progressed, could only watch from the landing as Osbert, Nanny and Mrs Brinkhoff carried the family's few remaining possessions up the seven flights of stairs to their new home.

—⋅—

Nanny's apartment was every bit as grim as Osbert had imagined from the outside. The pipes rattled behind the walls, and rainwater dribbled in through the ceiling and onto Osbert's bed. The window was so high that he could not easily look outside. Only by placing a box against the wall was he able to reach up and look out. It reminded him painfully of Mr Lomm's basement cell at The Institute. The walls were as damp, the wallpaper was rotting and the air was full of the same fusty smell of mould. He thought back over the tumultuous events of the previous weeks. His parents had lost their home, his father had been dismissed from the bank and Mr Lomm was gone. It seemed that nothing would ever be right again.

Osbert buried his head in the pillow and cried himself to sleep.

CHAPTER SIX

————◆◆◆◆◆————

THE FOLLOWING morning Osbert woke early. His room was hot and stuffy, and the fetid stench from the glue factory filled the air, making him feel sick and dizzy. He reached up on the box to open the window. In the doorway of a crumbling apartment across the street, a fat man in a dirty grey vest was playing a trumpet. Osbert watched him.

'What are you looking at?' shouted the man. 'Stare at me like that again and I'll come over and cut your liver out.'

Osbert jumped down from the window and ran out into the sitting room. Nanny was already up, frying duck eggs for breakfast on the ancient kitchen stove.

'There's a man across the street who says he's going to cut my liver out,' said Osbert.

'He's always saying that,' said Nanny, grinding pepper on the eggs. 'I always say to him, you can't cut my liver out if I cut yours out first.'

Mrs Brinkhoff emerged from her bedroom. Her face was pale and her hands shook.

'Whatever's wrong?' asked Nanny.

'It's Mr Brinkhoff. He won't get out of bed. He won't say a word to me. He just lies on his back, staring at the ceiling.'

'We best call for the doctor,' said Nanny. 'Many's the man who refuses to get out of bed for duck eggs who's dead and cold before lunch.'

Doctor Zimmermann arrived an hour later. He spent a long time examining Mr Brinkhoff. When at last he closed the bedroom door and stepped out into the kitchen, his brow was furrowed.

'Is he very ill?' asked Mrs Brinkhoff.

'An attack of the nerves,' said Doctor Zimmermann.

Mrs Brinkhoff smiled uncertainly. 'But he will get better, won't he?'

'Difficult to say,' replied the doctor. 'If he was still living in his apartment on Marshal Podovsky Street I should say with bed rest and nourishing bowls of soup he should be better within a fortnight. But here, in the Old Town, with the foul air and the stench from the glue factory...' Doctor Zimmermann stopped himself and clicked his tongue.

'The best you can do for the man is to keep him warm and comfortable and try to prevent any unnecessary shocks that might further unbalance him.'

That afternoon, Osbert went for a walk in the cemetery. He always found that it was a good place to think, and now that the Brinkhoffs were living in Nanny's apartment it was only a short distance away.

Osbert was reluctant to return to his new home, to the suffocating fumes from the glue factory and the man across the street who wanted to cut out his liver. Instead, he decided to explore the cemetery further, leaving the footpath and pressing on through the tall grass to investigate the tombs that lay beyond.

On and on he walked, until he became aware of a large and imposing structure of grey slate. It was a curious building that seemed to resemble The Institute, though it was many times smaller. It had no windows and the doorway was sealed shut, covered with a thick layer of green moss. The light was beginning to fail, and only by squinting through the gloom could Osbert make out the inscription: *Erected by subscription in memory of the tutors of The Institute.*

The building was a mausoleum.

Beneath the lichen, beside the doorway, there was more writing, and by gently peeling back the moss, Osbert discovered dedications to long-dead teachers from The Institute carved into the cold slate walls. It was curious how many of them had met grisly and untimely deaths. Osbert was familiar with the story of The Institute's great benefactor, Julius Offenbach, who had boiled to death in his bathtub, but there were tales the boy had never heard before, illustrated by a frieze, portrayed in relief at the top of the mausoleum. There was an epitaph for a teacher who had drowned in the River Schwartz when his motor launch struck rocks and sank, one for a teacher who had fallen from the battlements of the Governor's Palace, another for a teacher who had been torn to pieces by wolves while picnicking in the woods beyond the city walls. All in all, the history of The Institute had not been a happy one.

Osbert sighed, lost in thought. He knew who was responsible for his family's misfortune. Deep in his heart he hoped that Fate would grant his former teachers the same unlucky ends as their predecessors.

A week later, Mr Brinkhoff rose early. He made a pot of coffee and rye-bread toast and sat at the kitchen table reading the morning edition of *The Informant*.

'You're well again!' cried Osbert, hugging his father tightly.

Mr Brinkhoff laughed and patted Osbert on the head.

'Perhaps you should go back to bed after breakfast,' said Mrs Brinkhoff, who was not quite so convinced that her husband had made a full recovery.

'But after breakfast I'm taking Osbert into the city.' He smiled, a broad grin that Osbert had not seen in weeks. 'Today, my dearest wife, I am going to buy Osbert a new violin.'

'We don't have any money,' said Mrs Brinkhoff calmly and quietly.

'Oh, but we do,' replied Mr Brinkhoff, taking his wife's hand and squeezing it gently. 'Enough for a violin, I'm sure. I've had a bit of luck, you see!'

But this was not strictly true – luck never smiled on the Brinkhoff family any more. Mr Brinkhoff had raised the money by pawning his brown patent shoes and selling his favourite coat of Brammerhaus tweed.

The violin shop was in the artisan quarter of the city, close to the Imperial Railway Station. It was a small and elegant shop, with case after case of violins and cellos, polished to an exquisite shine; they seemed to glow like burnished gold behind the glass of the wooden display cabinets. There were new bows, paper packets of violin strings, plaster busts of Schwartzgarten's great composers and conductors – the little shop was so full, it was almost impossible to walk from one end to the other without knocking something over. A round and entirely bald man with half-moon spectacles stood on a ladder, sorting through sheaves of sheet music. He nodded to his two customers.

'Brinkhoff, isn't it?' said the man.

'I'm surprised you remember me,' said Mr Brinkhoff, greatly moved.

'And this must be your son,' said the shopkeeper, climbing down from the ladder.

'Yes,' replied Mr Brinkhoff. 'This is little Osbert'.

'And will Osbert be requiring a new violin, just like his father?' asked the shopkeeper.

'I haven't played the violin since I was a boy,' said Mr Brinkhoff sadly. He had not played a note since he had failed his examination for The Institute, and was startled to see just how expensive violins had become.

'Might you,' inquired Mr Brinkhoff, 'perhaps have some less expensive violins?'

'Maybe I have,' said the shopkeeper, smiling kindly and disappearing through the back door of the shop.

When the man returned, he held in his hand an ancient and battered violin case. 'This is the cheapest violin we have,' he whispered to Mr Brinkhoff. 'I'm afraid it isn't in very good condition. It's yours for five crowns.'

Mr Brinkhoff opened the case and peered inside. The instrument contained within was barely recognisable as a violin; the neck was splintered, the tuning pegs were missing and the strings were snapped.

'Thank you,' said Mr Brinkhoff. 'We'll take it.'

'Very good,' said the shopkeeper, wrapping the case in string and brown paper to prevent it from falling apart.

Osbert's heart sank. Returning home with his father, Osbert placed the instrument in Nanny's cupboard, still tied in its paper wrapper. Such a violin could surely never be repaired.

That night, while Osbert slept, Mr and Mrs Brinkhoff secretly retrieved the package from the cupboard and set to work restoring the violin. Every night for three weeks they sat together at the kitchen table by the light of Nanny's oil lamp. Mr Brinkhoff carved new tuning pegs, glued the neck of the violin back into place and attached new strings. Finally, Mrs Brinkhoff polished the wood to a brilliant shine; the violin glowed a dark amber colour in the guttering lamplight.

The instrument was complete.

———❖———

When Osbert woke the next morning, reaching across to retrieve his spectacles from the chair beside the bed, his fingers touched the battered violin case, which Mr Brinkhoff had placed there many hours before. Hardly daring to hope, Osbert sat up in bed and pulled the case onto his lap. His heart beat heavily in his chest. He flicked the catch on the side of the case and held his breath. There inside was his violin; not the ravaged and splintered wreck his father had bought from the music shop, but the most beautiful instrument he had ever seen. It was even more beautiful to Osbert than the Constantin Violin.

There was a knock at the door, and Mrs Brinkhoff entered with a glass of lingonberry cordial and a gingerbread biscuit.

'Is it what you wanted?' asked Mrs Brinkhoff, who was not at all musical.

'Yes,' said Osbert. He was so happy he could hardly speak. 'Can I practise my scales for Father? Where is he?'

'In bed,' said Mrs Brinkhoff. 'He's staring at the ceiling again. I think he may have over-exerted himself repairing the violin. I'm sure he'll be quite well again, in a day or two.' But the anxiety in her face betrayed the lie.

* * *

That evening, hugging the violin tightly to his chest, Osbert set out for Professor Ingelbrod's Academy. As he had been expelled from The Institute, Osbert was no longer entitled to a place at the Academy, but he could not let the day pass without showing Isabella his precious instrument.

'Is it a *new* violin?' asked Isabella curiously as she waited outside the Academy with her fellow students while Professor Ingelbrod unlocked the ancient mahogany door.

Osbert smiled. 'Not new,' he whispered, 'but the most wondrous instrument ever.'

Professor Ingelbrod, who had not noticed Osbert in the crowd, turned suddenly and inhaled sharply, as though sniffing out a disagreeable odour. Hunting for the source of the smell, his gaze soon fell on Osbert.

'We have one student too many,' he hissed. 'One student who no longer has a place in the Academy.' He grasped Osbert by the arm and pulled him through the door of the building, dragging him up the stairs to the music room. Isabella and her fellow violin students followed behind in a stupefied trance.

Osbert stood shakily at the front of the room and Professor Ingelbrod jabbed him sharply in the chest with his bony finger. 'What are you doing here, Slack-spine? Speak, boy. Speak!'

'I came to show Isabella my violin,' whispered Osbert.

'But you don't *have* a violin,' smirked the Professor. 'The bailiffs came and took it away, didn't they? And without a violin, what could you possibly be doing here?'

'I *do* have a violin,' said Osbert, opening his violin

case and proudly displaying the instrument his parents had worked so hard to repair. Unable to lean forward because of his back corset, Professor Ingelbrod bent slightly at the knees so he could observe the instrument more closely. He extended a bony hand and picked up the violin by one of its strings.

'This?' said the Professor, peering closely at the instrument. 'What is this?'

'It's my new violin,' replied Osbert.

'Look! Look everybody!' sneered Professor Ingelbrod. 'Osbert Brinkhoff has a *new* violin!' He seized the neck of the violin and flung it with force against the wall, so hard that the beautiful instrument shattered and buckled.

'If you are not a student at The Institute,' snarled Professor Ingelbrod, 'then you don't belong here either, do you? Now leave this place at once!'

Osbert picked up the shattered shell of his violin, placed it carefully inside the case and closed the lid. His heart felt shattered too, smashed to shards in the hollow of his chest. But he did not cry. He would not give his grinning, vindictive tutor the satisfaction.

As Osbert stepped into the street outside the Academy, he heard Professor Ingelbrod screaming at Isabella through the open window of the music room.

'No good, no good!' snapped the Professor. 'Your fingers,' he observed, 'are too weak, too short. They must be strengthened and lengthened, so they are long and agile like mine. Let this be a lesson to you. A lesson to all of you!' And with that he led Isabella from the room, where her beautiful music would no longer distract his students.

Osbert knew what fate lay in store for Isabella. Professor Ingelbrod would take her down to the cellar, where he would carry out his cruellest punishment. Taking two lengths of violin wire, the Professor would tie Isabella's fingers together, securing the ends of the strings to a pair of rusting meat hooks, which he had screwed securely into the cellar ceiling. Poor Isabella would be forced to stand on her own in the dark, her hands raised above her head as the wire violin strings stretched her delicate fingers.

Osbert stood in the street, his face burning with anger. What could he do? He would not let Isabella suffer on her own, tied up in Professor Ingelbrod's dark and mouldering cellar. Osbert waited until he heard the Professor return to the music room above. He turned the door handle and crept back inside the building. Upstairs, Ingelbrod's students were playing a short composition that the Professor himself had written, entitled 'The Raven Is A Nightmare Bird'.

Osbert descended the staircase to the cellar. Down and down he climbed, until he reached the dark oak door at the foot of the stairs. Cautiously, he turned the handle and opened the door. There stood Isabella, balanced on tiptoe, her fingers suspended from violin strings, tied in neat bows to the meat hooks in the ceiling.

'You came back for me?' said Isabella, as Osbert loosened the strings and released her.

'I'll always save you,' said Osbert, as he took Isabella by the hand and led her back up the dark staircase to safety.

Together they fled Professor Ingelbrod's Academy, as the sound of violin music scratched and whined from above.

The day after rescuing Isabella from Professor Ingelbrod's clutches, Osbert was idly passing his time in the cemetery before returning to his grim new home for a meagre supper cooked up by Nanny on the gas stove.

The cemetery was home to a number of scrawny half-starved cats that lived among the crumbling vaults and memorials. Osbert sat stroking a skeletal ginger tomcat he had named Bag-of-Bones, and thought again about life in Nanny's apartment. He thought about the noise of the rats in the attic above that kept the Brinkhoff family awake at night and the scuttling cockroaches that had shredded his mother's nerves. He thought sadly about his father, who never smiled any more. And then he began to think about Professor Ingelbrod; how cruelly he had punished Isabella, and how heartlessly he had destroyed the precious violin. And the more he thought, the harder he stroked the bony ginger cat, until the creature hissed angrily and ran off through the deserted cemetery.

As he sat in silent contemplation, the germ of an

idea entered into Osbert's brain. It festered and grew until it became a plan; a plan that made him glow with warmth, despite the coldness of the day. He would be avenged of Professor Marius Ingelbrod.

That night, as Nanny and his mother and father slept, Osbert slipped from his bed and dressed silently. Tiptoeing across the floor of the apartment he quietly opened the door, leaving it on the latch so he could return later. Walking swiftly along the streets of the Old Town, Osbert made his way over the Princess Euphenia Bridge, through Edvardplatz and towards Professor Ingelbrod's Academy.

It was midnight by the time Osbert reached the Academy, and he could hear the dull rumble of the great Schwartzgarten bell as it marked the hour from the Emperor Xavier clock tower. The street was in darkness, apart from a glimmering pool of light cast by a guttering candle in the Professor's dining-room window. Osbert stalked silently over the cobblestones. He was about to peer in through the window, when the door was suddenly flung open and a figure appeared from inside. It was Professor

Ingelbrod's housekeeper, Mrs Zukov. Osbert pressed himself against the wall, disappearing into the shadows.

'Not a word of thanks I get,' muttered Mrs Zukov, tying a scarf around her head. 'I cook and I clean for the old devil, and you'd think I was invisible for all the thanks he gives me.' She slammed the door behind her, clattered down the steps and made her way up the street, all the time muttering under her breath. 'Well, let him enjoy his supper, and I hope it chokes him, the poisonous old goat.'

Osbert waited until Mrs Zukov had rounded the corner at the end of the street. He emerged from the shadows and crept back to Professor Ingelbrod's window, cautiously peering inside.

The Professor sat alone at the dining-room table, enjoying the frugal supper of cheese, cracker biscuits and anchovy paste that Mrs Zukov had prepared for him.

Osbert stood patiently, watching the man eat. It was a revolting sight. The Professor's face was so thin that, as he chewed, the muscles on either side of his jaw began to swell, bruising his brittle, pallid skin.

Finally, Professor Ingelbrod rose from the table and by the light of a candle made his way out of the room and up the stairs to bed, carrying the remains of his supper with him on a wooden tray, to which he added a glass of milk and a lump of butter, to see him through the night. His limbs were as long and spindly as the legs of a harvester spider, and every step he took brought with it an orchestrated chorus of cracking bones and clicking muscles, which Osbert could hear clearly through the windowpane.

Osbert waited until Professor Ingelbrod had disappeared at the top of the stairs, then silently made his way up the steps to the front door. He had fashioned a skeleton key from an untwisted paperclip, and was preparing to pick the lock when he noticed that the door was ajar. Mrs Zukov had slammed the door so hard that it had sprung open again. It seemed to Osbert that Fate was smiling on his nocturnal enterprise. Gently pushing the door open, he entered the Academy.

There was enough moonlight filtering in through the dining-room window to guide Osbert to the foot of the stairs, but as he climbed up to the second floor of the building every step carried him further into pitch-blackness. The upper windows of the Academy were shuttered, and it was only Osbert's memory that enabled him to make his way from room to room in the darkness. At last, silently stepping into the music room and slowly picking his way past the rows of music stands, Osbert found what he was looking for. There, in Professor Ingelbrod's desk drawer, was a large reel of violin string. Placing the string in his jacket pocket, Osbert crept out of the room and along the landing, where he climbed the stairs to Professor Ingelbrod's bedroom.

Pushing the door open a crack, Osbert slipped inside. Ingelbrod lay in bed, asleep. The candle still flickered on the table by the window, casting Osbert's shadow high against the wall.

Professor Ingelbrod grunted and snorted in bed, his spindly limbs flailing like those of a dying insect, and came to rest on his back. His eyes flickered for a moment; he gave another snort, then lay motionless, deep in sleep. And as he slept, Osbert took the reel of violin string from his pocket and tied Professor Ingelbrod's fingers and toes to the great iron bedstead, one by one, until the teacher was securely pinned into place.

When Osbert's work was complete, he leant carefully over the sleeping figure of the Professor. There was no sound. Not even a hoarse rattle of breath. Osbert was beginning to wonder if the man was dead, when suddenly, with a lizard-like movement, Professor Ingelbrod's eyes blinked open.

'Who's that?' he demanded. 'Who's there?'

Osbert stepped back into the shadows. The Professor could make out the size of the figure, but not the face.

'What are you doing here, boy?' he demanded. 'Show yourself, Slack-spine!'

Professor Ingelbrod attempted to climb out of bed, but he could not move. Looking down, he was alarmed to discover that every one of his fingers and toes had been tied to the bedstead with violin string. It was as though he had been cocooned in the web of a giant spider.

'Untie me,' he barked.

But Osbert had no intention of untying the man. It was important that the teacher should learn his lesson. And as the Professor had taught him so well, lessons were to be learnt the hard way.

As quietly as he had entered Professor Ingelbrod's Academy, Osbert let himself out, pulling the front door closed behind him until he heard the latch drop back into place. Smiling at a job well done, he walked quickly along the moonlit street and headed home.

CHAPTER SEVEN

I T MUST be said that the tragedy that befell Professor Ingelbrod occurred entirely by chance. Osbert had not intended to kill the man, but to teach him a lesson he would remember until the end of his days. Of course, he could not have predicted just how few of those days the Professor had left.

Osbert had imagined that Professor Ingelbrod's housekeeper, Mrs Zukov, would arrive the next morning and, discovering her employer tied to the bedstead with violin strings, would release the man. But this did not happen. It did not happen because Mrs Zukov was not in Schwartzgarten to rescue him. She had travelled on the early morning express train to visit her sister for a ten-day holiday in the mountain town of Obervlatz.

When, for the seventh evening in a row, the Professor failed to open his door to the students of the Academy, the matter came to a head.

Osbert and Nanny, who were out for an evening walk, were curious to find a crowd had gathered outside the building. The shutters had been crowbarred away from the windows, and a ladder had been placed against the wall.

'Whatever's happened?' asked Nanny.

'Take a look and see,' said Mrs Mylinsky, whose husband had provided the ladder.

Nanny didn't have a head for heights, so she stood at the bottom of the ladder as Osbert slowly climbed the rungs to the second storey of the building.

The tiny windowpanes were smeared with years of grime, so Osbert took his pocket handkerchief and wiped the dirt from a small circle of glass. It was dark inside the room and it took time for his eyes to grow accustomed to the gloom. On a table in front of the window the candle had burnt down to a stub. The milk had curdled; the butter was rancid in its dish. A rat scuttled across the floor. Slowly, Osbert was able to make out distinct shapes at the other end of the room; the washstand and basin, the woodworm-riddled hulk of a carved oak wardrobe, and there, stretched out on the bed, the grey, lifeless figure of Professor Ingelbrod, somehow even greyer in death than he had been in life.

Naturally, Osbert had been curious to know what had become of Professor Ingelbrod; but never in his wildest imaginings had he considered the possibility that the man was dead.

It was an hour before the Inspector of Police and the Coroner arrived by motorcar, and during that time the crowd outside the Academy had swollen to such an extent that it was impossible for the car to pass along the narrow street. All the time the curious citizens of Schwartzgarten had been taking it in turns to climb Mr Mylinsky's ladder and peer in at the withered corpse of Professor Ingelbrod.

The Inspector was a round and serious man with a drooping moustache, who had no time for ghoulish sightseers. He stood on the steps of the Academy, the wizened Coroner hunched beside him, peering myopically at the crowd through a pair of gold-rimmed spectacles.

The Inspector blew his whistle. 'If you spent a little less time gawping at the body, and a little more time smashing down the door, perhaps we might get to the bottom of all this.'

The crowd were more than eager to smash down Professor Ingelbrod's door. But it was a substantial door, and it took some minutes before the great slab of ancient mahogany finally buckled. Swinging on its twisted brass hinges, it crashed to the ground, the iron door knocker giving one final thud before being silenced forever.

The crowd watched impatiently as the Inspector and the Coroner stepped over the fallen door and into the stale air of Professor Ingelbrod's hallway. Cautiously, they climbed the staircase and disappeared from view.

———

When the Coroner emerged from Professor Ingelbrod's house twenty minutes later, he shook his head and waved his finger at the assembled crowd. 'Professor Ingelbrod is most assuredly dead.'

Nanny pushed to the front of the crowd, dragging

Osbert behind her. 'And what was it that killed the Professor?' she cried.

'The man was murdered,' grinned the Coroner. 'He has been tied to the bedstead with violin string and starved to death.'

The Coroner waved his hands in the air and a battered motor hearse, which had been parked discreetly in a side street, slowly approached the Academy. At the wheel of the hearse sat Schroeder the undertaker, dressed in a faded black mourning suit and dusty black top hat, reeking of cough syrup and beetroot schnapps. Schroeder sounded the horn at intervals to clear the street of onlookers.

As the hearse shuddered to a halt, the undertaker tumbled out onto the pavement, clinging to the side of the vehicle to keep himself upright.

'You're drunk,' snarled the Coroner.

'And *you're* a midget,' growled the undertaker. 'Murder, is it?'

The Coroner nodded.

Schroeder banged his fist on the back of the hearse and the door swung open. A young man, painfully thin and dressed in a black suit two sizes too large, stuck out his head.

'Yes, Dad?'

'Murder,' smiled the undertaker. 'We'd best take the smartest stretcher. There's a crowd out here, so let's give them a show.'

The Professor was carried out on Schroeder's most ornate stretcher, his body covered with a crisp white sheet. But as Schroeder and his son descended the steps, the undertaker (still suffering from the effects of beetroot schnapps) lost his footing and slipped backwards. The Inspector of Police leapt forward to break the undertaker's fall, but it was too late. As Schroeder fell, so too did the stretcher. The crowd gasped in horror as the body of Professor Ingelbrod slid out from beneath the sheet, his grey skeletal fingers still tied with neat bows of violin string.

That night, Osbert sat alone in his bedroom and considered the day's events. It was impossible to forget the image of his lifeless violin teacher; it was forever lodged in his memory.

He could not completely comprehend the feelings that consumed him. Pity? Remorse? It was neither of those things. The feeling which welled up from the pit of his stomach was something quite different. It was excitement. Excitement, and deep satisfaction.

———

Professor Ingelbrod's funeral was held the following Monday. The Principal had declared an official half-day of mourning, and as a mark of respect the shops that lined the route from the mortuary to Professor Ingelbrod's final resting place were forced to close, their windows obscured by black velvet blinds.

It was a bitterly cold morning, and Nanny and Osbert slipped and slid as they walked the frozen streets of Schwartzgarten. They waited on the corner of Alexis Street, outside the museum, and at a quarter past nine a clattering of hooves on the icy cobbled street heralded the arrival of the funeral party. Professor Ingelbrod's coffin was transported in a glass bier, pulled by two black horses with braided manes. Behind the carriage came a procession of students from The Institute, all dressed in black and kept in line by Mr Rudulfus, who barked orders from the rear of the party.

Osbert watched his former classmates silently, his features rigid in the freezing air. But his eyes were alive, like two marbles moving watchfully inside the frozen mask of his face.

Nanny leant over and whispered in Osbert's ear. 'There she is, Osbert. There's your little friend.'

And there was Isabella, almost obscured from view by the stout frame of Doctor Zilbergeld. Isabella's white skin looked even paler against the black of her dress, and for a moment Osbert feared that she might be ill. He coughed, hoping to attract Isabella's attention, and sure enough the girl caught his eye, just a flash, a half-smile, enough to show Osbert that she knew he was watching.

Behind Doctor Zilbergeld, the procession continued. Shrouded in black came the remaining tutors of The Institute. First was Anatole Strauss, puffed up with his own self-importance and relishing every moment of the mournful occasion. He was followed by Mr Rudulfus, struggling to keep up with the party, scuttling along the street like a tiny black beetle; a beetle Osbert would have happily stamped on and squashed. Last, but certainly not least, came the Principal, beating rhythmically on the ground with the tip of his Malacca walking cane, looking for all the world like the figure of Death, stalking his prey.

Osbert and Nanny were not alone on the pavement. They had been joined by another onlooker; the Inspector of Police. He was a troubled man. He had no clues. No suspects. No leads at all.

Of course, Ingelbrod's housekeeper, Mrs Zukov, had been questioned, but it soon became clear that she was not the culprit.

'If I done it, don't you think I'd be *proud* to say I done it?' she said. 'Whoever done for him, did us all a favour. Poisonous old goat, he was.'

'Upsetting for the boy,' whispered the Inspector to Nanny, observing Osbert's solemn expression as the funeral party passed out of sight.

But it was not the Professor's death that troubled

the boy; Osbert was only upset by the fact that he had killed Professor Ingelbrod by accident and not by design.

—◆—

The following day, Osbert returned to the cemetery. He no longer needed to follow a pocket map; he knew his way around the graves and monuments as well as he knew his way along the streets of Schwartzgarten itself. His feet crunched through the frozen grass as he headed towards the mausoleum.

He ran his hand across the entrance to the vault. Stripped of lichen, it was cleaner than he had ever seen it, exposing a Latin carving he had never noticed before: *Memento Mori.*

'Remember you must die,' he whispered.

He looked up at the names of his former teachers, already engraved on the mausoleum in readiness for their eventual demise. The Principal was a scrupulously tidy man, and as the tutors invariably continued to teach at The Institute until the day they expired, it seemed wise to add their names to the grave in advance. Even the

Principal's own name had been engraved, embellished in gold leaf. The only name that was absent from the list was that of the kindly Mr Lomm, which had been replaced by a pristine slab of grey slate, forever erasing the tutor's name from memory.

'I thought you'd be here,' said a quiet voice.

Osbert turned and there stood Isabella.

'Hello,' said Osbert.

Isabella smiled. She jumped up onto the tomb of Marshal Biedermann, and sat silently, swinging her legs backwards and forwards.

Osbert did not know what to say. He was worried that Isabella would be able to read his face; that she might tell at once that he was to blame for the death of their respected violin teacher. Osbert smiled sadly and attempted to appear innocent of the crime. 'It's very unfortunate about Professor Ingelbrod.'

'Do you think so?' replied Isabella, without a moment's hesitation.

'Don't you?' asked Osbert, curiously.

'No,' said Isabella and paused, kicking her feet thoughtfully against the tomb. 'In fact,' she continued, 'if every last teacher at The Institute were to die horribly, they'd only have themselves to blame, wouldn't they?' She turned and stared directly into Osbert's eyes, melting his heart though the day was bitterly cold. 'I know you agree, Osbert.'

She smiled an odd smile, and jumped down from the tomb, singing to herself as she walked off through the cemetery, leaving Osbert all alone with his dark thoughts.

Osbert took Isabella's place on the tomb of Marshal Biedermann, and stared hard at the mausoleum before him. It seemed to pose an interesting question. What if some disaster should befall each of his former teachers? A disaster that should result in them joining Professor Ingelbrod inside the great mausoleum, sooner than nature had intended.

Osbert carefully contemplated matters. The history of Schwartzgarten was an undeniably bloody one; would he be making matters *much* worse by adding to the bloodshed? If anything, surely, he would be enriching the history of the great city?

Osbert considered this prospect and his mind

wandered to the chemistry teacher, Doctor Zilbergeld. If another 'accident' were to occur, he could not think of a more deserving candidate.

CHAPTER EIGHT

———◆·✕·◆———

DOCTOR ZILBERGELD was a large woman, with black hair so tightly pulled back into a bun that it looked as though it had been painted on. The pungent smell of the chemicals she mixed in her laboratory hung everywhere about her; on her clothes, her skin, her breath. Sulphur had yellowed her fingernails, which she concealed beneath a thick layer of scarlet nail polish.

Isabella stared from Doctor Zilbergeld's classroom window onto the courtyard below. Although she was sure the sun was shining, there was no glimmer to be seen through the smeary glass panes. The only signs of flora and fauna in the courtyard were the choking weeds, a patch of orange fungus and an emaciated grey rat, which emerged from the window of the basement room that had once belonged to Mr Lomm. Isabella often wondered what had become of her former tutor. As she cast her mind back to the happy days when Mr Lomm once taught her, she was rocked from her daydreaming by a sickening screech, as Doctor Zilbergeld ran her red painted fingernails down the blackboard. Isabella turned suddenly.

'You.' Doctor Zilbergeld pointed a fat finger at Isabella. 'Tell me the answer.'

But Isabella could not think of the answer, because she had not heard the question. She sat mutely.

'Say something!' barked the Doctor.

It was as though every single word had drained from Isabella's head. Doctor Zilbergeld slammed her chalk on the table, so hard that it shattered in a cloud of dust. She advanced on Isabella, seizing her by a tuft of hair and pulling her, screaming, to the front of the class. Doctor Zilbergeld seemed to delight in torturing poor Isabella, and had already pulled out so much of the girl's hair that she had left bald patches in several places.

It was high time, thought Isabella, that another murder took place.

When Osbert met Isabella in the cemetery that evening, beneath the sharpened blade of the Grim

Reaper's scythe, Isabella held out a small box. Inside was a tuft of hair tied in a bright red ribbon.

'*My* hair,' explained Isabella, 'that Doctor Zilbergeld pulled out. I thought you might like it. So you'll always think of me.'

'I will always protect you,' said Osbert quietly. 'I'll take our secrets with me to the grave.'

He held the box tightly. No more words were exchanged between the two friends. No words were necessary. Osbert and Isabella were undoubtedly in agreement: something had to be done about Doctor Zilbergeld.

———

The following afternoon, as Osbert and Isabella sat in the café of the Myops' pastry shop eating gingerbread macaroons and sipping from glasses of iced lingonberry cordial, they watched in fascination as Doctor Zilbergeld entered the shop.

Mrs Myop wheeled the pastry trolley to the Doctor's table. It almost groaned under the weight of silver and gilt cake stands. There were chocolate tortes, brittle pastry shells piled high with sugared cloudberries and confectioner's custard, coffee éclairs and a glittering tower of crisp choux pastry buns smothered in a thick caramel sauce.

'That one, there,' said the Doctor, pointing at a plump slice of golden apple and cinnamon strudel. 'Give me that one.'

Mrs Myop obeyed, then retired to safety behind the shop counter. With a flash of polished silver, Doctor Zilbergeld cut into the strudel, displaying all the skill of a surgeon as she neatly dissected it with her pastry fork. The caramel was crisp and not too sticky, the apples were moist but not too soft. But something was wrong. She sighed and pushed the plate away, dabbing the corner of her mouth with a napkin.

She suddenly became aware of Osbert watching her.

'You, boy! Don't I know you?' she croaked.

'Yes, Doctor Zilbergeld,' said Osbert.

'Of course,' replied the Doctor. 'You are the Mylinsky boy, am I correct?'

Osbert felt as though the air had been knocked

from him. How dare Doctor Zilbergeld mistake him for Milo Mylinsky?

'You are not correct,' said Osbert, with pride in his voice.

'Don't contradict,' snapped the Doctor. 'If I say you are the Mylinsky boy, then that is exactly who you are.'

Osbert was preparing a response when Doctor Zilbergeld rose from her table and left the shop without paying her bill, her red leather shoes clattering over the cobbles.

Mr Myop shook his head. 'Never eats a whole slice of strudel. It's enough to break a baker's heart.'

'But you make the best strudel in the city,' said Isabella.

'Not to Zilbergeld. Nothing compares with the Oppenheimer Strudel Factory.'

The Oppenheimer Strudel Factory had closed three months before, and in Mr Myop's opinion, it was then that the steel really entered Doctor Zilbergeld's heart. He showed Osbert and Isabella a postcard of the factory, and on the back the Oppenheimers' legendary recipe for apple and cinnamon strudel.

Doctor Zilbergeld lived in a house on her own, beyond Edvardplatz and close to Schwartzgarten's Imperial Railway Station. It was a tall building, but unusually narrow, with one room on each of its six floors. Many people wondered how a house so thin could possibly contain a woman so fat.

It was such a thought that occupied Osbert as he set off for home in the Old Town, having spent an hour spying on Doctor Zilbergeld from an empty house across the street and making notes in his pocketbook.

On the corner of Doctor Zilbergeld's street stood the premises of Oskar Sallowman, the chicken butcher. Since his earliest childhood, Osbert had been fascinated by the shop. He loved the smell, the colours, the chance to see the flash of the silver meat cleaver as it sparked and glinted from the dark recesses of the shop.

For Osbert's fourth birthday he had been given a wooden model of a butcher's shop, with a tiny metal cleaver (carefully blunted), a set of scales that actually worked and sides of meat made from pieces of painted plaster. Osbert would sit and play all day, chopping at the painted pieces of meat with the blunt steel cleaver.

Oskar Sallowman the chicken butcher was a great, greasy mound of a man. He strode like a giant across the cobbled streets of Schwartzgarten, his breath cracking the air in painful rasps.

'He eats children,' Mrs Mylinsky had told her horrified son, Milo, 'and grinds the bones to dust.'

'That is nonsense,' Mr Mylinsky had added. 'He eats the children, bones and all.'

But Osbert never believed the stories. After all, if everyone knew that the butcher ate children, surely the police would have been called?

As Osbert walked past the shop of the chicken butcher, he noticed a sign in the window: *Wanted: Apprentice. Afternoons only.*

Osbert smiled at the unexpected opportunity that had presented itself. Working in the butcher's shop would provide him with the perfect cover to spy on Doctor Zilbergeld, and whatever wages he earned could help to support his impoverished parents.

Stepping past the large cockroach that staggered,

bloated, through the open doorway, Osbert entered the lair of Oskar Sallowman.

It was a small shop, smelling of blood and chicken grease. As Osbert walked across the sawdust-scattered floor he passed row upon row of plucked chickens, hanging in neat lines from long iron bars, suspended from the ceiling. Oskar Sallowman stood at the chopping block, sharpening his knives.

'What do you want?' said the butcher, eyeing Osbert suspiciously.

'Good afternoon, Mr Sallowman,' said Osbert. 'I have come about the job.'

The man shifted on his feet. The veins at the side of his great bald head seemed to throb as his scarlet face became a deeper shade of crimson. The butcher began to laugh, wiping his hands on his bloodied apron.

'Job!' he roared, bending down to look Osbert in the eye. 'How old are you, boy?'

'Eleven,' replied Osbert, then he added quickly, 'but I'm nearly twelve.'

Mr Sallowman observed Osbert closely, his hot breath crackling out of him, rancid with chicken fat and garlic. The smell was so strong that Osbert could feel his eyes watering.

'Come with me,' said the great butcher, striding through to the back room of the shop. Nervously, Osbert followed him. 'You're hungry?' the man asked.

'Yes,' said Osbert, hungrily.

'You look half-starved,' said the butcher. A pan of thick chicken soup bubbled on the stove, and Oskar Sallowman took a ladle, stirred the thick broth, and poured out two bowls of the steaming liquid. 'What do your parents think about you becoming a butcher's assistant, eh?' said the man, handing Osbert the bowl of soup and a spoon, which he first wiped on his apron.

'I haven't asked them,' replied Osbert.

'Just our little secret?' asked the butcher.

'Yes,' said Osbert.

They sat and ate their soup in silence, as the butcher thought things through. The boy was small, but he was eager, that much was clear. And there was something in his eye, something that convinced Sallowman that butchering was in Osbert's very soul.

'It doesn't pay much,' said Oskar Sallowman at

length. 'And I like a boy who's quick at learning.'

'I won't disappoint you,' said Osbert.

'You'd better not.' The butcher sat back in his chair, draining the last dregs of the chicken soup and mopping up the smears with a dry crust of bread.

'You do lessons, I suppose. Book learning and the like?'

'Yes,' replied Osbert. 'But only in the mornings.'

'What will you tell your parents?' asked Sallowman. 'If I decide to give you the job?'

Osbert thought for a moment. 'Every afternoon I shall tell them that I've gone for a walk in the cemetery,' he said.

'Do that often, do you?' asked the butcher with a smile.

'I do,' replied Osbert.

'Very well,' said Oskar Sallowman. 'You can start tomorrow afternoon, as soon as your lessons are over.'

———◦———

Osbert was as good as his word, and learnt the job quickly, sweeping the sawdust from the floor and scrubbing down the wooden counter. Blood was in his lungs and beneath his nails. At the end of each afternoon he would wash his hands in the sink, watching as the blood curled down the plughole. And then Oskar Sallowman would pour Osbert a steaming cup of the thick chicken soup, and together they would sit in the back room and talk.

'There's love in killing,' said Mr Sallowman one afternoon, as he opened the door of the hen coop to survey the clucking, squawking birds that had been delivered to his shop that morning. 'Love and hate all rolled together as one.'

He was a tender-hearted killer. Gently, he took the chickens from their perches, stretching their necks and neatly cutting off their heads with the blade of his gleaming cleaver. Osbert watched in awe as Oskar Sallowman filleted the chicken carcasses, cutting out the gizzards, livers and hearts, plying his trade with brutal efficiency. He threw the feathers and innards into a smouldering barrel in a corner of the yard beyond the shop, filling the air with a thick fog of suffocating black smoke. In under an hour the butcher's yard, once full of the sound of squawking poultry, fell entirely silent.

The silence was shattered by the furious jangle of a bell. Sallowman raised his head, and his lips curled into a snarl.

'That woman!' he growled, brushing feathers from his apron and wiping his bloodied hands in a damp cloth. He lumbered off into the shop.

Osbert followed Oskar Sallowman inside. There, beside the counter, stood Doctor Zilbergeld. The air was ripe with the Doctor's perfume, Oil of Marshflower, the only scent powerful enough to cover the sulphurous stench of chemicals from her laboratory at The Institute. In her hands she clutched a small cardboard box.

'What do you want?' asked Sallowman.

Without a word, Doctor Zilbergeld lifted the lid of the box and held up a brittle caramel pastry.

'Well?' grunted Sallowman.

'Smell!' demanded Doctor Zilbergeld.

Oskar Sallowman's nostrils twitched. He could smell nothing but chicken flesh and the cloying, sickly sweet aroma of Oil of Marshflower. He stared blankly at Doctor Zilbergeld and shrugged his shoulders.

The Doctor's cheeks burned the colour of sour cherry jam and she hissed, a noise like an exploding gas pipe.

'Chicken!' barked Doctor Zilbergeld. 'It smells of *chicken*! Chicken and burnt feathers. You're filling the air and polluting my pastries!'

'A man has to earn a crown or two,' said Sallowman pathetically.

'A man can't earn a curseling, let alone a crown,' growled Doctor Zilbergeld. 'Not if he's out on the street. And that's *precisely* where you'll end up if Anatole Strauss has his way. You're living here on borrowed time, Sallowman.'

She closed the lid of the pastry box and stormed from the shop, trailing the heavy scent of Oil of Marshflower as she disappeared from sight.

'Bad things should happen to that woman,' said Sallowman as he shut up the shop and paid Osbert for his afternoon's work. 'May her life on this earth be a short one.'

These were Osbert's sentiments exactly. Of course, Doctor Zilbergeld was not a young woman, and she had already spent a long life on earth. But Osbert was determined that she should not outstay her welcome.

That night, alone in his room above the shop, Oskar Sallowman sat down to compose an anonymous letter. He burned with rage.

Doctor Zilbergeld, he began. *You're the one polluting the air with that evil-smelling perfume you splash on.* He smiled; the letter was going well. *Another thing,* he continued, enjoying every word as it formed on the page, *speak to me again like you did today and I'll fillet you like a chicken, you poisonous great hen.*

———

For a time, Osbert was happy. The money he earned was carefully divided between two jars, which he hid under the loose floorboard beneath his bed. One jar was marked *Mother and Father* and the other *War Chest*.

Osbert's birthday was fast approaching and Mr and Mrs Brinkhoff, though now very poor, were still anxious to celebrate to the best of their ability. The question arose of a suitable present to mark the special day.

'What would you like *most*?' asked Mrs Brinkhoff.

'A hunting suit and cape,' replied Osbert. 'If it's not too expensive.'

And so, the next day, Mr and Mrs Brinkhoff took their son to the tailors Hempkeller and Bausch.

'Good morning,' said Mr Bausch. 'How may I assist you?'

'In two weeks,' said Mr Brinkhoff, 'Osbert will be twelve, and he has expressly asked for a hunting suit.'

There was a rattle of brass curtain rings, and Mr Hempkeller appeared from behind the velvet curtains at the back of the shop.

'Ah, Mr Hempkeller,' said Mr Bausch. 'Young Master Osbert Brinkhoff's parents wish to procure for him a hunting suit for the occasion of his twelfth birthday.'

'Quite right, quite right,' replied the ancient tailor courteously. 'Every child worth his salt should be fitted for a hunting suit. Brammerhaus tweed, perhaps? A fine twill in green would suit Master Osbert Brinkhoff *admirably.*'

'I must have pockets,' whispered Osbert to his father. 'Many pockets.'

'Of course,' said Mr Bausch. 'What is a hunting suit without pockets?

'If Master Osbert would be so good as to step up here,' said Mr Hempkeller, uncoiling a long tape measure. 'Bending makes my bones crack.'

Osbert climbed up onto the counter and stood patiently as the tailor took measurements.

'Don't forget the pockets, please,' insisted Osbert.

'What manner of devilry is little Osbert planning, I wonder?' said Mr Hempkeller with a smile.

Politely, Osbert returned the smile.

———

In order to pay for the suit, it was decided that Mrs Brinkhoff would have to take a job. Mr Brinkhoff had rallied a little, and felt capable of looking after himself in the afternoons while his wife took a part-time secretarial position at the glue factory. It was a miserable place to work, and every evening when Mrs Brinkhoff returned home to Nanny's apartment she would carry with her a miasma of poisonous glue vapours, which made her sick to the stomach.

'It's a wonderful place to work,' said Mrs Brinkhoff, her face puce and her eyes bloodshot.

'You don't look well, Mother,' said Osbert. 'Are you sick?'

Mrs Brinkhoff shook her head. She gathered up all her strength and smiled. 'I'm well,' she replied. 'And more than that, I'm happy. Mr Lindersoll says I am the glue that holds the factory together.'

Of course, this was not the truth. She hated every second she spent peering through the fog of glue fumes as she typed letters for the brutish Mr Lindersoll, who was slow to praise his unlucky employees and always quick to find fault.

But Mrs Brinkhoff kept her thoughts to herself, and every day she would tell her son how much she loved her work, how kind and gentle Mr Lindersoll could be, and how the stench of glue was as sweet to her as perfume. She loved Osbert and so she lied to him, in the hope she could make him happy.

───•─•───

When Osbert awoke on the day of his twelfth birthday, there was a brown-paper parcel waiting for him on the kitchen table. Nanny made pancakes and hot cocoa as Osbert unwrapped the present. He smiled.

'My hunting suit!' He kissed his mother and father, and ate his breakfast hungrily.

That afternoon, as Osbert swept the sawdust and chicken feathers from Oskar Sallowman's shop, the butcher called him into the back room.

'Happy Birthday, Osbert,' said Mr Sallowman, and held out a small package wrapped in newspaper and tied with string, pressing it into Osbert's hand. 'Open it, boy.'

Osbert's nimble fingers swiftly ripped open the paper, and inside he discovered a small cleaver, so small as to sit snugly in his clenched fist. It was a beautiful cleaver, a brilliant cleaver, reflecting the light from the dull yellow ball of grime that rose above the rooftops and passed for sun in the gloomy city of Schwartzgarten.

Oskar shut up the shop, and Osbert returned home to a supper of Nanny's duck-egg soufflé. The Brinkhoffs could not afford a birthday cake, so they sat at the table and shared a bag of salted caramels. That night, as the house slept, Osbert stood in his bedroom admiring himself in front of the full-length mirror. His hunting suit was more beautifully tailored than he could have dared to hope. He had brown leather boots, a green twill suit and the new hunting cape. Most importantly, the cape and suit were full of pockets.

Osbert took out his new cleaver and held it to the light, watching as it reflected beams of silver onto the walls and ceiling. Opening one of the pockets in his hunting cape, he carefully placed the cleaver inside.

He smiled. The time had finally come for Osbert to put his plans into action.

CHAPTER NINE

⬦

THE FOLLOWING Saturday morning, Osbert unfolded his map of Schwartzgarten. There, in the southernmost reaches of the city, marked in black ink were the words: *Oppenheimer Strudel Factory*.

The sun glowed a murky orange in the cold, grey sky as Osbert pushed his way through the crowds, hurrying to the end of Anheim Street, where he bought a tram ticket to the industrial quarter of Schwartzgarten.

It was easy enough to find the old factory, with its glass roof and towering apple silo. The doors were locked and the windows boarded. Osbert took a pin from his pocket book and inserted it in the padlock on the factory gate. He carefully wiggled the pin around, and the padlock clattered to the ground. He walked across the factory yard and cautiously entered the deserted building, squeezing behind a sheet of corrugated iron loosely nailed over a window.

Inside, the factory was in darkness. Osbert smiled. The automated strudel machinery lay undisturbed, exactly as it appeared on the postcard Mr Myop had shown him, perfectly preserved behind the locked and bolted door.

<hr />

'Will you show me how to make apple strudel?' asked Osbert.

'Why?' said Isabella suspiciously.

'Because I want to know how to make it,' said Osbert.

Isabella finished sweeping the floor of her father's pastry shop. 'What's it worth?' she asked.

'I'll be your faithful friend until we're both dead and buried,' said Osbert.

Isabella frowned. 'I meant, something that's worth something. Like chocolates.'

'I don't have any chocolates,' said Osbert.

'Then you'll have to owe me,' said Isabella, her eyes sparkling at the thought.

Osbert watched as Isabella weighed out butter and flour, and set to work kneading and rolling the pastry until it formed elegant and wafer-thin leaves, the way her father had taught her.

'I wonder if there'll be another death sometime soon,' she asked innocently as she cored the hearts from the apples, chopping the fruit and scattering the pieces across the buttered pastry.

'There might be,' said Osbert. 'I suppose we'll have to wait to find out.'

Isabella giggled, folding the strudel pastry and slashing it neatly with a knife.

'I suppose bad things always happen to bad people,' said Isabella.

'I suppose you're right,' said Osbert.

Isabella opened the oven door and slid the strudel inside.

'But what about ingredients?' asked Osbert. 'I'd need flour and apples, and other things. If I want to make it myself, I mean.'

'Enough for one strudel?' asked Isabella.

Osbert shook his head. 'A lot more than that,' he replied.

Isabella grinned. 'I'll ask my father to order more.'

'What will you tell him?' asked Osbert.

'I don't know,' said Isabella. 'That I'm making strudel for the poor little ones at the Schwartzgarten Reformatory for Maladjusted Children.'

'Isn't that stealing?' said Osbert.

Isabella shrugged. 'I don't suppose so,' she said.

But Osbert was not convinced. 'Will he believe you?' he said, doubtfully.

'My parents believe everything I tell them,' said Isabella, grinning.

Every night for a week Osbert sat at the desk in his bedroom, poring over intricate diagrams of the strudel machinery, making detailed drawings in his pocket notebook of cogs and ratchets, levers and pulleys. And little by little his knowledge grew.

Isabella was as good as her word. The ingredients arrived two weeks later. Mr and Mrs Myop were delighted to discover that their daughter was devoting her time to charitable work.

As Doctor Zilbergeld climbed into bed, taking a final bite of a plump cherry pastry studded with delicious nuggets of almond marzipan, she made a note in her school ledger. The next morning she was resolved to make the life of Isabella Myop even more unbearable than usual. It was a happy thought, and the Doctor smiled to herself, wiping the last crumbs of pastry from the corners of her mouth. She had noticed that the girl had become more absent-minded as the weeks had gone by, and this suggested that Isabella had a dangerous spark of imagination. If there was one thing the Doctor detested most, it was children with imagination. As she lay back in bed, pulling the counterpane tight around her fat neck, she imagined tugging so hard at Isabella's hair that the girl's head became separated from her neck. She smiled drowsily, and began to snore.

She had been asleep for little more than two hours when she was suddenly awoken by a banging at the window. She sat up in bed and listened. Somebody was throwing stones. She jumped from her bed and rushed to the window. She could see nobody on the street outside. There was another thud. The stone seemed to cling to the glass, defying the laws of gravity. On closer inspection, she could see that it was not a stone at all; it was a lump of golden marzipan. Putting on her dressing gown and slippers, she rushed downstairs and opened the front door. There at her feet was a white cardboard box, wrapped with a bow of black ribbon. As she tugged at the bow, a delicious aroma seemed to escape from inside the box. It was a smell she remembered well. A sweet scent of fresh, buttery pastry and baked apples. Doctor Zilbergeld lifted the lid to reveal a mouth-watering slice of plump apple strudel, with a crumbly streusel topping of sugar and cinnamon. The pastry was light and brittle, and as she took her first bite the strudel seemed to dissolve on her tongue. She closed her eyes and sighed ecstatically. Quickly devouring every delicious, sugary morsel of the strudel, Doctor Zilbergeld discovered a message at the bottom of the pastry box. Plainly written in neat red ink were the words: *The Oppenheimer Strudel Factory is once again open for business, and welcomes Doctor Zilbergeld.*

The Doctor hurried back inside the house to fetch

her hat and coat and her red leather gloves.

It was two o'clock in the morning and the streets of Schwartzgarten lay silent as Doctor Zilbergeld hurried along the deserted avenues and alleyways. She walked past the Imperial Railway Station, and on towards the industrial district of the city. Doctor Zilbergeld gasped and wheezed her way up to the top of the hill. In the distance was the unmistakable outline of the Biedermann Anchovy Paste Works, with the large golden anchovy hanging above the entrance gate. The street lamps threw out little light, but there before her, at the bottom of the hill, was the building she had often revisited in dreams, with its soaring brick walls and enormous glass roof. The Oppenheimer Strudel Factory.

Doctor Zilbergeld almost ran down the hill in her excitement. She ran through the open gates and into the factory yard. Towering high above her stood the wooden apple silo, partly obscured by a cloud of smoke, which belched from the factory's spindly chimney, seeming to solidify into a great grey ball in the cool night air. There was no doubt about it; the factory was once more in business. Hanging from the door was a freshly painted sign: *Doctor Zilbergeld, the Oppenheimer Strudel Factory is honoured by your arrival. We fondly hope you have a large appetite.*

But there was nobody to greet her. Nobody answered when she rapped her fist against the door. The factory lay silent, apart from the distant hiss of machinery from within.

'What sort of a welcome is this?' she muttered under her breath.

Pushing the door she found that it opened easily. There was a scurrying noise in the darkness.

'Rats,' she hissed. 'Filthy creatures.'

She rattled the inner door, terrified that the rats would get to the pastry before she could. Her lungs were so full of the smell of apple and cinnamon she thought they might burst. A light filtered from under the factory door and Doctor Zilbergeld tugged frantically at the handle, desperate to get inside. It was only by pressing her full weight against the door that she was able to force the lock open. And what a wondrous sight she beheld. It was as though the clocks had been turned back and the Oppenheimer Strudel Factory had never closed its doors. The pistons hissed and pounded, driving the mighty machinery on the factory floor. Apples tumbled from the high wooden silo, before being washed and sliced, mixed with spice and sugar, and folded into the wafer-thin sheets of strudel pastry. Doctor Zilbergeld clapped her hands and shrieked with delight. But as the shriek carried and echoed back at her through the vast building, she realised that something was not quite right. She was entirely on her own in the factory.

'Hello?' she called. 'This is Doctor Zilbergeld. Is this the way you treat your honoured guests? Show yourselves at once.' She heard a scampering on the floor behind her. 'Rats,' she spat. 'Rats everywhere!'

But she was mistaken; there were no rats. It was simply Osbert, silently clipping an iron hook to the belt of Doctor Zilbergeld's coat. Before she had a chance to utter another word, the Doctor felt herself being lifted from the ground. She gazed up in horror and saw that she was suspended from a rope, which was winching her rapidly towards the darkness of the apple silo, high above the strudel machinery. The pulley creaked and groaned as Osbert hoisted the Doctor ever higher into the wooden tower on the mechanical winch.

'What's going on?' she cried. 'Who's doing this? Stop it at once or you'll be sorry!'

But there came no reply.

Many dark thoughts whirred through Doctor Zilbergeld's mind as she lurched upwards. Would her unseen assailant drop her to her death on the concrete floor below? Would she be left suspended in the tower to starve to death? The rope gave an elastic bounce as the pulley squealed to a halt. Beneath the Doctor's dangling feet the doors of the silo slid into place.

⎯⎯◆⎯⎯

Every day, as soon as his work for Oskar Sallowman was done, Osbert would make his way across the city of Schwartzgarten, as far as the tram would take him. Then he would walk to the Oppenheimer Strudel Factory to visit Doctor Zilbergeld, suspended from her rope in the apple silo.

The silo was so tall that it projected through the

glass roof of the factory, and it was as wide as a tram is long. Osbert had to climb a ladder to peer in at his captive through the small hatchway in the side of the tower. And every afternoon, as Doctor Zilbergeld swung round in the darkness, the wooden door of the hatchway would creak open on its hinges. Then a spoon would appear, tied to the end of a long walking stick – this was the easiest way Osbert could find to feed the Doctor. From the gloom of the silo, Doctor Zilbergeld could not make out Osbert's face as he spooned her full of strudel.

There was strudel of infinite variety, and sometimes sweet-cherry dumplings, chocolate torte and crisp sugared pastries. Doctor Zilbergeld was powerless to resist the delectable desserts. And as Osbert fed the Doctor, he recited the verse that Nanny sang every night at supper.

'One for the banker,
Two for the clerk,
Three for the beggar
who sleeps in the park.'

With every spoonful she ate, Doctor Zilbergeld

became a little fatter. Osbert fed the teacher until she was so fat the rope groaned and stretched under her enormous weight.

CHAPTER TEN

THE TEMPERATURE had dropped. The Department of Police was as cold as an ice house and the Inspector sat huddled at his desk, warmed only by the feeble heat from an ancient electric fire. He was a troubled man. What had become of Doctor Zilbergeld? He was waiting for inspiration to strike, which of course it did not. His brain was numbed by the cold.

People were beginning to wonder if the Inspector of Police was equal to the challenge of finding the woman. He had failed to track down Professor Ingelbrod's killer, what hope was there for Doctor Zilbergeld? The Inspector's wife was so ashamed of her husband that she had thrown him out of the house and changed the locks. As a consequence, he was reduced to sleeping on the worn and creaky sofa in his office, in little more comfort than the prisoners in the cells below.

'I think,' said the Inspector, hauling himself out of his chair and lighting a cigar, 'we should pay another visit to Doctor Zilbergeld's house. See if there's anything we've overlooked.'

But a thorough re-examination of the Doctor's house offered few clues.

'Perhaps she's gone on holiday?' suggested the Constable.

The Inspector of Police opened Doctor Zilbergeld's wardrobe. 'But all her clothes are here,' he sighed. 'I think it's time to fetch Massimo.'

Fearfully, the Constable made his way out into the street, opened the police wagon and disappeared inside. There was a loud roar which seemed to rock the wagon, and a shriek from the Constable, who reappeared dragging a long chain behind him. At the end of the chain was a jet black Doberman, the name *Massimo* engraved on his heavy iron dog collar.

The dog growled and snapped at the Constable's ankles. 'Get the scent, boy,' whispered the Inspector, tickling Massimo behind the ear and holding out one of Doctor Zilbergeld's overcoats. Massimo's tail stopped wagging and the dog whined miserably as he breathed in the sickly aroma of Oil of Marshflower.

Massimo had no interest in following such a revolting smell. Instead, he led the Inspector and the Constable to the park, where he ran around happily sniffing at lampposts.

Still Doctor Zilbergeld ate. Every mouthful of apple strudel she wolfed down seemed more delicious than the last, until she was very nearly apple-shaped herself.

It was in the second week that the rope began to break. Every day Osbert had made notes in his pocketbook about the state of the rope: how many strands had frayed, how the increased weight of Doctor Zilbergeld had lengthened the rope. The more the Doctor ate, the more the rope frayed. But she was powerless to save herself. She knew that if she did not eat the strudel she would undoubtedly starve to death, and she had no intention of doing that.

And then, on the thirteenth day, the strain on the frayed threads of rope became too great. Osbert had arrived early with a batch of freshly baked pastries. He climbed the ladder and was preparing to open the flap in the side of the apple silo, when he heard a desperate moan and a series of loud thumps. Lifting the hatch he was surprised to see Doctor Zilbergeld, still suspended, attempting to run around the inside of the silo, like a cyclist in a velodrome. To begin with Osbert could not understand why she was doing this. His teacher had never shown any interest in exercise. And then he noticed that Doctor Zilbergeld was only suspended by a single thread of the rope. She had somehow managed to swing herself over to the wooden wall of the silo; by running along the riveted iron band that ran around the circumference of the tower she was lessening the strain on the rope, which sagged and was no longer pulled taut. But all she could do was run; the iron band was not nearly wide enough for her to stand upon, and calamity was unavoidable if she lost her footing, as the sudden pull on the rope would undoubtedly snap the remaining thread. Osbert was impressed; he had not suspected this streak of ingenuity in the Doctor. For a moment he almost pitied her, but then he remembered

Isabella, and the tufts of hair Doctor Zilbergeld had pulled from his friend's beautiful, blameless head. He let the hatch swing shut, and raced downstairs to the factory floor.

Disaster was inevitable and duly came. Hallucinating from frantic exercise and too much strudel, Doctor Zilbergeld imagined that she was transforming into a mighty bird. She stretched out her arms and flapped, expecting to take flight, soaring up towards the roof of the apple silo, where she would burst through the rafters and fly home. And as she pondered this majestic thought, she lost her footing, slipped from the wall and swung down into the centre of the silo. She reached out frantically, clutching at the walls, but this only made her spin faster at the end of the rope. And the faster she spun, the quicker the rope began to fray, until finally, with a twang like a rubber band snapping, the rope gave way, exactly as Osbert had planned. Doctor Zilbergeld shrieked as she plummeted from the tower, snapping the brittle doors of the hatch below like sugar biscuits and dropping onto the well-polished apple chute, which lay directly beneath the wooden tower. As she slid down the mirror-smooth metal, she attempted to slow her descent, trying desperately to dig her shoes into the side of the chute. But the metal was polished to such a shine that she continued to slide quickly towards the waiting conveyor belt below, where she landed in a crumpled and quivering heap. There, beside the great machine, stood Osbert.

'You,' gasped Doctor Zilbergeld.

Osbert nodded.

'Little Milo Mylinsky.'

'No,' said Osbert, patiently. 'My name is Brinkhoff. Osbert Brinkhoff.'

Doctor Zilbergeld stared at the boy in bewilderment. 'Do I know you?'

Osbert could feel the blood surging through his head. He fought to contain his anger.

'Yes, Doctor Zilbergeld. I was a student at The Institute. Then I was cheated of the Constantin Violin and expelled.'

'Ah,' grunted Doctor Zilbergeld. 'Of course. It all comes back to me now.'

'And you were cruel to Isabella Myop. You pulled out tufts of her hair.'

'Shouldn't have had it so long, should she?' snarled Doctor Zilbergeld. 'But enough of this,' she rubbed her hands victoriously. 'Now, Brinkhoff, if that *is* your name, you must come with me to the Department of Police.'

Osbert pressed a switch. Quietly at first, the cogs of the strudel machine began to grate and turn; the machinery was slowly shaking itself into life.

'What…what's happening?' spluttered Doctor Zilbergeld.

She attempted to stand; attempted, but could not. The conveyor belt began to move, throwing her onto her back and tossing her into a large metal drum – the apple steamer. As the drum slowly revolved, the Doctor was doused with jets of hot water and turned cherry pink in the clouds of steam. She shrieked as a rotating arm of tiny spinning blades slowly lowered from above, slashing at the apples, peeling and shredding them; the blades were not sharp enough to kill the Doctor, but scratched her skin and ripped her clothes. With a hiss of pistons, a hatch opened in the bottom of the drum and Doctor Zilbergeld was dropped into an enormous metal mixing bowl, twice as wide as the apple steamer and three times as deep. Osbert climbed a ladder and scattered in handfuls of shredded apple, which rained down on the Doctor.

'Get me out of here, boy!' she shrieked, climbing unsteadily to her feet.

'No,' replied Osbert, pulling a lever.

As Doctor Zilbergeld was scraping chunks of apple pulp from her hair, she became aware of an ominous groaning of machinery. Looking up, she was in time to see a wave of melted butter as it poured into the mixing bowl from a vast aluminium bucket, sluicing her onto her ample behind. She had hardly recovered from this indignity when she was showered with an appetising downpour of sugar and raisins, cinnamon and lemon zest and ground almonds. The bowl began to rotate, mixing the ingredients for the strudel filling. Doctor Zilbergeld was bumped and bashed until, with a sudden upwards jerk, the mixing bowl was raised into the air and tipped on its side, depositing the contents back onto the conveyor belt. The belt felt softer than before, and seemed to sink beneath Doctor Zilbergeld as she crawled forward on her hands and knees. She sneezed, and disappeared for a moment in a cloud of flour. Suddenly, all became clear to the Doctor; she had landed in the middle of a large square of strudel pastry, sticky with apricot jam. From above, a blanket of pastry was dropped into place and Doctor Zilbergeld gave a muffled yelp as she was pinned in position by the mechanical pastry roller, an enormous cylinder of bright polished steel. Her arms flailed as she tore at the pastry, ripping an air hole and panting for breath.

'Brinkhoff!' she screamed, as her head emerged from beneath the pastry shroud. Wiping sugar and butter from her eyes, she became dimly aware of a flashing of silver at the end of the conveyor belt.

'The strudel-slicer!' she gasped.

'Yes,' replied Osbert. 'The strudel-slicer.'

'Help me,' cried the Doctor as she was carried rapidly along the conveyor belt. But there was nobody to come to her aid. Only Osbert Brinkhoff, who had no intention of helping her. He surveyed Doctor Zilbergeld solemnly, as she was dragged from the conveyer belt towards the waiting jaws of the strudel-slicer.

'You will go to Hell!' screamed Doctor Zilbergeld.

'Perhaps,' observed Osbert calmly. 'But you'll get there first.'

Doctor Zilbergeld had freed her arms and head from the shroud of pastry and made a valiant effort to claw herself away from the rapidly revolving blades, which glinted like silver in the daylight flooding through the enormous glass roof of the factory.

But the ripped and flapping corner of her jacket had become snagged on the cogs of the machine, which tugged at the pastry, pulling it inch by inch from the conveyor belt towards the spinning blades of the strudel-slicer.

Osbert was amazed by the Doctor's sudden show of speed as she slipped her arm from her jacket, attempting to escape before the iron teeth of the cogs could snap at her and crush her fingers. She held up her hand triumphantly, her face glazed with sugar and perspiration. Osbert watched in horror as she turned to face him.

'You see?' snarled Doctor Zilbergeld. 'I'm free. Now you're in trouble!'

But Doctor Zilbergeld's triumph evaporated in the twinkling of an eye. As if making an enormous effort, the machine roared and screeched, and the cogs slowly turned, trapping the other sleeve of her jacket as it tugged the pastry onwards. Once more she tried to squirm free, but it was too late; her fate was sealed. As she wriggled and fought to release herself, her skirt also caught in the machinery, dragging her into the embracing mouth of the industrial slicer. It appeared at first that the blades would buckle under Doctor Zilbergeld's monumental weight; the cogs creaked and groaned; they seemed to lose their grip. But little by little, Doctor Zilbergeld was devoured by the machine, until all that could be seen were the very tips of her pointed red leather shoes. There was a single, ear-splitting scream, and then nothing.

'Good boy, Massimo,' said the Inspector of Police, as the Doberman came to a slavering halt outside the Oppenheimer Strudel Factory. The Constable leant against the wall, out of breath and wheezing asthmatically. 'This must be the place,' continued the Inspector, flinging Massimo the steak that had enticed the dog to follow the scent. 'Whatever has happened to Doctor Zilbergeld has happened here.'

The Inspector of Police had not expected to find Doctor Zilbergeld alive, but he had at least hoped to discover her in one piece. But the Doctor had been chopped into many *hundreds* of pieces – a nose here, a finger there – all wrapped in delicious golden pastry, sprinkled with cinnamon and dusted with confectioner's sugar.

'Looks like she's written something, Inspector,' said the Constable, pointing at the tiled wall above the conveyor belt of the strudel machine. 'It's hastily done, but the word's clearly scrawled for all to see.'

'The poor unfortunate woman was about to be slashed into bits by the strudel-slicer,' said the Inspector. 'I think we can forgive her if her handwriting was a little untidy.'

The Constable bowed his head apologetically, and Massimo seized his moment to bite the man hard on the back of the leg.

'Quiet,' said the Inspector, as the Constable's scream rose up to fill the cavernous factory. 'It seems as though the writing's been done in jam.' He held his finger to the wall, wiped away a sample of the sticky preserve and tasted it. 'Apricot.' He clicked his tongue, deep in thought.

'But what does it mean?' said the Constable, staring at the daubs of jam, and massaging his leg. '*OS?*'

'Initials, I shouldn't wonder,' said the Inspector. 'Perhaps our evil mastermind is growing careless.' He smiled. 'And nobody applauds a sloppy murderer. She's all yours,' he said, waving his hand to the Coroner, who stood patiently in the shadows, bucket in hand.

The following morning at breakfast, Osbert sat reading *The Schwartzgarten Daily Examiner*. The front page carried a photograph of Doctor Zilbergeld and beneath it the headline: SLAUGHTERED TEACHER LEAVES VALUABLE CLUE SMEARED IN APRICOT JAM.

Osbert folded the newspaper and slowly sipped his glass of lingonberry cordial. He could not believe that he had been clumsy enough to provide the police with such an important clue. He was determined never to make such a mistake again.

That night, Osbert let himself out of the apartment, a wooden box safely tucked under his arm. He walked the street along the north bank of the River Schwartz, slinking into the shadows whenever he heard voices, or if he spotted a passing policeman. He made his way to the Grand Duke Augustus Bridge, and opened the box. Inside were the tools of his secret trade, among them the reel of violin string which he had used to tie Professor Ingelbrod to the iron bedstead, the instruction manual he had read to work the Industrial Strudel Machine and one of his old pocketbooks. It was all evidence, and every bit of it incriminating.

By the light of the street lamps, Osbert hauled the wooden box onto the parapet of the bridge and pushed it over the side, watching as it was tossed around in the surging waters below before being swept downriver towards the forest beyond Schwartzgarten.

—◆—

It took the Coroner the next three days to gather

together the tiny, bloodied pieces of Doctor Zilbergeld from the strudel factory. On the death certificate he wrote: *Sliced to bits and baked.*

Under cover of darkness, the Coroner drove the pieces back to the undertaker's shop, contained in eighteen metal buckets in the back of his motor hearse. He drove gingerly over the cobbles to avoid slopping out the contents.

After two weeks, working late into the night, Schroeder had done his best to sew the little fragments of Doctor Zilbergeld's body back together. Even with many parts still missing, the body was so heavy that when it was loaded into the motor hearse the engine would not start; it merely spluttered and ground to a halt, leaking oil in a sticky pool on the cobblestones. Instead, the Principal arranged for a legion of thirty boys to carry Doctor Zilbergeld's body to the mausoleum.

The smell of apple and cinnamon, which wafted from the coffin, was so overpowering that each and every boy vowed never to eat another mouthful of strudel as long as they lived. The procession was joined by a pack of stray dogs, howling wildly and licking up any dribbles of strudel syrup that seeped from inside the coffin.

Doctor Zilbergeld was a vile and violent woman, yet her funeral was well attended by the citizens of Schwartzgarten. This was not out of pity, but relief. They were anxious to see the Doctor safely interred in her final resting place.

Isabella Myop watched as the door to the mausoleum was sealed shut. Her eyes darted around the assembled mourners – there seemed to be somebody missing. Where was Osbert Brinkhoff? Isabella had been sure that her friend would attend the funeral. But there was no sign of the boy.

As the crowds departed the cemetery and swarmed through the Gate of Skulls, Isabella was almost trampled by the sea of mourners and could feel the life being crushed out of her. But as she struggled to keep her footing she felt someone reach out and press an envelope into the palm of her hand. She could not make out who it was, although she was certain she saw the flash of a green twill hunting cape as the figure moved away, swallowed up by the surging crowd.

Isabella set off for home. Crossing the Princess Euphenia Bridge, she stopped to examine the mysterious envelope. On the front, written in small but elegant handwriting, were just two words: *A memento*.

Opening the envelope, Isabella discovered a crisp shard of strudel pastry. She smiled knowingly, and continued home.

It was upsetting for Osbert to read through *The Informant* and *The Schwartzgarten Daily Examiner*; nobody had yet reached the conclusion that a genius was responsible for the killings. Osbert was determined to set the record straight. One night, when he put all thoughts of The Institute from his head and settled down in bed, Osbert took out a well-thumbed volume of short stories he had borrowed from Nanny and began to read. One story in particular arrested his imagination: *Wenceslas Wedekind, the Gentleman Poisoner*.

Wenceslas was a tall, elegant and ingenious murderer, who carried round a battered leather case containing vials of the most powerful poisons known to man. After despatching each of his victims (and there were many), Wenceslas would leave a calling card for his nemesis, Detective Dürnstein.

'Ah,' the Detective would mutter, pulling the calling card from the breast pocket of yet another corpse, 'The Gentleman Poisoner has struck again.'

Osbert smiled and climbed out of bed. He stole into the sitting room, where Nanny snored violently from the sofa, tangled in a blanket. Osbert quietly opened a drawer and took out Nanny's supply of blank calling cards, held in a leather case, which she used to send out violent threats in her tiny, neat handwriting when anyone crossed her. Osbert shuffled the cards carefully. There were twenty cards in all, more than sufficient for his grand scheme.

—◆—

Two days later, the Inspector of Police was nonplussed by the arrival of a small envelope, containing a single calling card. There was nothing written on the card, except for the letter *X* and the number *2*.

'Is it multiplication?' asked the Constable. 'Is the answer four?'

Massimo growled.

'Don't be a fool,' snarled the Inspector. 'It's the killer, that's who this is from. Times two. The killer's claiming responsibility for doing away with Professor Ingelbrod *and* Doctor Zilbergeld.'

That night, the late edition of *The Informant* carried the banner headline: WHO IS THE SCHWARTZGARTEN SLAYER?

'The Schwartzgarten Slayer,' repeated Osbert, proudly. He had achieved his goal – it was a sobriquet with which he was proud to be associated. As he cut out the headline and pasted it into his journal, Osbert's mind turned to his next victim.

———

It was a bitterly cold winter and the great River Schwartz had frozen over for the first time in fifteen years. The trees that lined the banks of the river were heavy with ice and the streets were grey with slush, churned up by the wheels of motorcars and the speeding trams, which seemed even more terrifying than usual as they loomed up suddenly through the clouds of freezing fog. Every week the newspapers carried stories of ill-fated pedestrians who had been concussed by a tram, or were unlucky enough to stumble on the cobblestones as one of the screeching and rattling vehicles rounded a corner, dragging them to their deaths beneath its wheels. It was little wonder that the citizens of Schwartzgarten affectionately referred to the trams as 'The Reapers'.

It was on such a Reaper, a week after the funeral of Doctor Zilbergeld, that Osbert made his way from the Old Town and into the city. Leather screens had been pulled around the open doors of the tram, to protect the passengers from the freezing blasts of wind and snow. The brim of the conductor's hat was white with sleet as he pushed through the crowded vehicle, punching tickets. But this was no pleasure trip for Osbert; he was spying on the Deputy Principal, Mr Rudulfus, who occupied the seat opposite him.

Osbert wore a cap, pulled down over his eyes and a muffler wrapped around his neck, so that he was almost invisible to his fellow passengers.

Mr Rudulfus was elegantly dressed in a neatly tailored suit with a silk cravat, a dark purple amethyst pin in a silver mount skewering the necktie in place. His high white collar was so stiffly starched that it appeared to slice into what little neck he had. There was nothing about Mr Rudulfus that seemed comfortable. Osbert had only visited the teacher's classroom on one occasion, but he had never forgotten it. It was a small room with an extremely high ceiling. Wooden cases lined the walls, filled with stuffed birds and animals from the forests beyond Schwartzgarten. A row of glass jars contained the internal organs of exotic beasts, preserved in formaldehyde, and a stuffed alligator hung suspended from a high shelf. Many of the animals had been chloroformed and despatched by Mr Rudulfus himself. Osbert shivered as he stared at the man.

Alarmed by the fluttering wings of a passing moth, Mr Rudulfus glanced up, his milky right eye darting blindly around the carriage. He swiped wildly with his umbrella, reducing the unfortunate creature to a cloud of shimmering dust. Settling back into his seat and reaching into his jacket pocket, he retrieved a small envelope, which he clutched tightly in his delicate fingers. In the dim light, Osbert could make out two Latin words scrawled on the front: *sub rosa*.

He carefully translated the words in his pocketbook: *in strict confidence*.

But what could the significance be?

The conductor punched Osbert's ticket as the tram rattled over the Princess Euphenia Bridge and into the city.

As Mr Rudulfus stepped down from the tram on the corner of Edvardplatz, Osbert climbed down behind him. The tutor was momentarily distracted by a raven as it cawed loudly from a rooftop above him, and Osbert seized his opportunity to drop a calling card into the man's coat pocket. He then followed Mr Rudulfus all the way to the Old Chop House.

The Inspector of Police was fearful that the Schwartzgarten Slayer would strike again and had demanded that the Old Chop House remain under guard. Osbert observed two police constables lurking outside as Mr Rudulfus entered the building and hurried upstairs to the dining room of the Offenbach Club.

Unable to follow his prey any further, and fearing that it would arouse suspicion if he lingered outside, Osbert reluctantly returned home.

The three remaining tutors of The Institute sat at the dining table, feasting on snails fried up in garlic, as they awaited the Inspector's arrival.

The mathematics teacher, Anatole Strauss, was attempting to scoop a particularly plump and succulent snail from its shell. 'Perhaps Doctor Zilbergeld's death will be the end of it?' he suggested optimistically.

The Principal snorted. 'An *end* to it?' he echoed, unpleasantly. 'Of course it won't be an *end* to it.'

'But what do you mean?' asked Mr Rudulfus.

'I mean,' replied the Principal, 'that somebody is deliberately trying to *kill* us. All of us.'

Mr Rudulfus dabbed his mouth with the corner of his napkin. Thoughtfully, he pushed one of the snails away with the prongs of his fork, only to watch it slide back on a slick of melted butter.

There was an apprehensive knock at the door.

'Enter!' demanded the Principal, and Anatole Strauss flinched, fearing that the knock heralded the arrival of the Slayer. But it was only the Inspector; his face pink and flushed.

He cringed. 'Apologies for my late arrival.'

The Principal glowered at the man. 'I trust it will not happen again.'

'Delicious-looking snails,' murmured the Inspector, who had not eaten, his stomach growling hungrily.

'They're gorged on milk until they're too fat to retreat inside their shells,' replied the Principal. 'Then we reward them for their gluttony by frying them to death in a pan of butter. And speaking of rewards…'

'Yes, yes, rewards,' said the Inspector. 'The Governor of Schwartzgarten has offered a reward of five hundred imperial crowns for information leading to the arrest of the Schwartzgarten Slayer. And it's the

Governor's opinion that the Festival of Prince Eugene should be cancelled this year.'

'Cancelled?' thundered the Principal. 'The most important festival in Schwartzgarten? *Cancelled?* I think not. This is our chance to smoke the Slayer out.'

Mr Rudulfus, who had just then reached into his pocket for a handkerchief, suddenly turned as grey as lead.

'What is it?' barked the Principal. 'What's wrong with you? Are you dying?'

'He's come for me,' gurgled Mr Rudulfus. 'The Schwartzgarten Slayer. I am to be corpse number three.'

He held out a small calling card, banded in black, which had been tucked inside the handkerchief.

'*X 3*,' he gasped. 'If the Slayer has come close enough to plant this card in my pocket, he has already come close enough to kill me.'

'Perhaps the card is a hoax,' ventured the Inspector. 'Maybe one of your students doesn't like you very much?'

'None of his students like him very much,' snapped

the Principal. 'That's the point of teaching.'

Though it felt as if rats were gnawing at his stomach, the garlic-drenched snails offered solace, so Mr Rudulfus continued to eat. He chewed rhythmically, consumed by terror.

'Yes,' continued the Principal. 'The Festival of Prince Eugene will take place, according to tradition. I think our friend the Slayer is growing too confident. He will make mistakes.' He gave a black-toothed smile. 'We need a tempting piece of bait to lure him into the open.'

'Bait?' asked the Inspector.

'The Star Box,' continued the Principal.

Mr Rudulfus gulped, almost choking on his last garlic snail.

CHAPTER ELEVEN

M R RUDULFUS had earned a reputation for eccentricity.

'There he goes,' people would whisper in the street, 'with his army of ravens.'

It did indeed seem as though the coal-black birds, which circled above the man as they followed his every footstep, cawing with near-diabolical delight, offered him some manner of supernatural protection. But this was far from the truth.

What Osbert did not know and could not possibly have known, was that Mr Rudulfus despised ravens with every ounce of his being, owing to an unfortunate incident in his early childhood.

One pale autumn afternoon many years before, as they passed the window of the furrier Alexis Haub, Mr Rudulfus's parents were momentarily distracted by a display of fur coats.

'A stole would be nice,' said Mr Rudulfus's mother,

enchanted by a silver fox fur wound round the headless throat of a tailor's dummy, its green glass eyes inviting her into the shop to buy it. And this she duly did, accompanied by her husband. The infant Rudulfus was left abandoned in his perambulator, with a paper bag full of millet for the family's pet parakeet. Attracted by the bag of millet, a raven flew down from the rooftop, its gnarled claws settling on the side of the pram; and there it perched, stabbing at the bag of seed with its razor-sharp beak.

When Mr Rudulfus's parents emerged from the shop minutes later, having forgotten altogether that they had a son in a perambulator, it was no longer daylight, or so it appeared. The sky had turned to pitch, but it was a sky the like of which they had never seen before. The air seemed to pulse and heave, and this it did with a disagreeable odour of rotten food and a thunderous chorus of cackles. Powerful black wings beat against the face of Mr Rudulfus's father, and an outstretched claw sliced at his cheek.

'Ravens!' he gasped.

But Mr Rudulfus's mother had troubles of her own.

The newly purchased silver fox fur had come to life around her throat, tugged by eight large ravens, which flapped madly, pulling the fur so tightly that it was choking the very life out of her.

A constable who happened to be passing the shop had the presence of mind to remove his gun from its holster, and fired twice into the air. The ravens took to the skies, wheeling wildly, crying out with a noise so unnatural it sounded for all the world like a curse.

As the last of the birds took wing from the pavement, the torn and tattered perambulator was finally revealed. There was not a noise from within. Not a burble, not a gurgle. Mr Rudulfus's mother peered inside, expecting to discover a bloodied pulp that had once been her son. But all that could be seen was a thick eiderdown of raven feathers, sprinkled with a few fallen grains of seed.

'He's gone! Eaten!' screamed Mr Rudulfus's mother. But a faint noise from beneath gave her hope. Frantically scraping away the feathers and the last grains of millet, she revealed the mewling form of her infant son.

'He's smiling,' she chirped, mistaking her son's terror for happiness. 'He's completely undamaged.'

Indeed, physically, the child was quite unharmed, but psychologically he was scarred forever.

Ever since that fateful day, it seemed that the birds could sense Mr Rudulfus's fear and thrived on it. Every morning, as he left his house in the Old Town, ravens would gather in the sky above him; one or two at first, until a murder of the birds had congregated, casting a dark shadow over the unfortunate teacher.

Every day *The Informant* printed letters from lunatics claiming to be the Schwartzgarten Slayer, while *The Schwartzgarten Daily Examiner* published editorials predicting that another gruesome murder was imminent. Throughout the city and the Old Town children had daubed the walls of shops and apartments with bright red paint: *Who is the Schwartzgarten Slayer?*

Many people were afraid to walk the streets at

night, in case the Schwartzgarten Slayer suddenly changed his modus operandi and began killing people indiscriminately, not just teachers.

Each morning the Inspector of Police rounded up possible suspects. The Governor of Schwartzgarten's offered reward of five hundred imperial crowns brought forward a wave of informants. Mrs Mylinsky reported her sister, who had a squint and looked the murderous type. Mr Freish reported the man who lived in the rented room above him and made too much noise with his wind-up gramophone (Mr Freish would have been happy to see the man hang, whether he was guilty of the murders or not). Nanny reported the fat man across the street who was always threatening to cut out people's livers.

One afternoon, as Osbert finished for the day at Oskar Sallowman's, he was alarmed by the arrival of the Inspector of Police, who walked to the back of the shop, where the butcher was wiping down his blades. The Inspector was followed by Massimo, dragging the Constable by the lead over the sawdust and chicken feathers.

'Are you Sallowman?' asked the Inspector.

'Who wants to know?' grunted the butcher.

'The Inspector of Police, that's who,' said the Constable, snapping handcuffs around the butcher's fat wrists. 'You're wanted in connection with the Schwartzgarten slayings.'

'On what evidence?' asked Sallowman.

'Death threats,' snarled the Inspector, taking a letter from the pocket of his overcoat and reading aloud. '"*Speak to me again like you did today and I'll fillet you like a chicken, you poisonous great hen.*" Seems you put that threat into practice, doesn't it?'

'It was a joke,' pleaded the chicken butcher. 'I didn't even mean to send it. Not really. Just a harmless joke.'

'Oh yes,' said the Inspector, nodding gravely. 'This is the Slayer all right. I'll stake my reputation on it.'

Osbert was left to shut up the shop. He felt sick at heart. What clues had led the Inspector to the door of his friend, the butcher? And then he remembered: the letters Doctor Zilbergeld had scrawled on the wall of the Oppenheimer Strudel Factory, *OS*. Had the Inspector mistakenly believed that they were initials? *O* for *Oskar*, *S* for *Sallowman*?

Guilt weighed heavily on Osbert's shoulders. How could he have been so foolish as to endanger his friend? He paced up and down his bedroom floor that evening, deliberating his next move. At dinner he stared mournfully at his mother and father. From early childhood the Brinkhoffs had impressed on their son the importance of taking responsibility for his actions and he did not want to disappoint them. His mind whirled. He could not allow Oskar Sallowman to be punished for the crimes that he himself had committed. And yet he could hardly give up on his master plan when he had come so far. But then what if Oskar Sallowman was executed for his supposed crimes? The thought became too much for Osbert to bear. Professor Ingelbrod and Doctor Zilbergeld had earned their fates, but the chicken butcher was blameless.

He had no choice. It was time to admit that he, Osbert Brinkhoff, was the Schwartzgarten Slayer.

——◆——

The new day dawned. The sky was leaden and the

cold rain seeped through Osbert's woollen overcoat as he trudged miserably towards the Department of Police.

He took a deep breath and pushed open the door. The only thought that lifted his sinking heart as he approached the desk sergeant was the certain knowledge that his confession would protect Oskar Sallowman from harm.

'Yes?' said the desk sergeant wearily, turning the pages of *The Informant*.

Osbert's throat was tight, and his voice escaped his mouth in a thin squeak. 'I have information about the Schwartzgarten Slayer.'

'Oh, yes?' said the desk sergeant with a wry smile. 'You're the killer, are you?'

Osbert was just about to reply that he was, when he noticed the headline on the front page of the newspaper: SALLOWMAN THE BUTCHER RELEASED.

'Is it true?' asked Osbert. 'Has Oskar Sallowman been released?'

'The man had an alibi,' said the desk sergeant. 'Pity. I was in the mood for a hanging.'

Osbert could feel a surge of relief race through his body.

'Well?' said the desk sergeant. 'What information have you got?'

'Nothing,' said Osbert hurriedly. 'Just that I thought Oskar Sallowman was innocent.'

'Just what you thought, was it?' said the desk sergeant, turning the page of his newspaper. 'Now clear out and stop wasting valuable police time.'

Osbert walked swiftly from the room and closed the door behind him. His legs shook and he had to steady himself against a wall, breathing slowly to control the beating of his heart. He had been moments away from disaster. Had he not seen the front page of *The Informant* he would have given himself away to the police and for no reason. But all was well. Sallowman was free and so was Osbert.

There was no such consolation for the Inspector of Police, who had staked his reputation on Oskar Sallowman's guilt. He barely slept that night, convinced that the Schwartzgarten Slayer was about to strike again. His wife still refused to let him come home.

Whenever he drifted off to sleep, the rusty springs of the office sofa would dig into his back and he would wake with a howl of pain, half-believing he'd been stabbed.

The next morning, his eyes tired and bloodshot, the Inspector sat at his desk, smoking a fat and stubby cigar. He stared brokenly at a collection of newspaper cuttings he had pasted into a large scrapbook. Each and every page was dedicated to the Schwartzgarten Slayer. Never had the Inspector seen a murderer work in such a deliberate and calculated manner. Could it be that the killer would spare the lives of Anatole Strauss, Mr Rudulfus and the Principal? The Inspector thought not.

Meanwhile, Osbert was occupied by the prospect of the impending Festival and, as the Inspector had correctly guessed, was looking for a festive opportunity to put an end to Mr Rudulfus.

One bright cold morning, Osbert and Isabella hurried towards the Governor's Palace, past the statues of the generals on horseback. Any citizen of the city was at liberty to visit the palace. The lower floors housed a grim yet fascinating collection of weaponry and exquisite instruments of torture, which charted the slow and painful unfolding of the city's bloody history. Osbert and Isabella looked up as they walked the marble floor of the Gallery of Traitors. The high-vaulted ceiling was decorated with an intricate design of spears, swords and arrows. The far wall was lined with a row of ancient suits of armour, one particularly grisly and rusting suit retaining the skeletal remains of its former occupant.

The gallery had earned its name from an ancient and unsettling tradition in the city of Schwartzgarten. After each beheading at the guillotine, the heads of unhappy traitors were slowly boiled down to remove the flesh, and the skulls were then burnished with silver and gold, and put on display as a warning to others. Of course, it was a tradition that had long since been abandoned, but the skulls still glittered and shone in the glare of the naked electric light bulbs which hung from the ceiling.

The Gallery of Traitors led through to a large central hall, containing a ramshackle assortment of busts and marble statues of Schwartzgarten's rulers and military leaders. The stories were familiar to Osbert.

'Who's that?' asked Isabella, staring at a large military portrait in a golden frame.

'General Daeneker,' replied Osbert. 'His father went mad and cut his head off.'

'And him?' asked Isabella, pointing at an alabaster bust on a shelf.

'That's Marshal Biedermann,' said Osbert.

Isabella smiled. 'Did something bad happen to him as well?'

Osbert nodded. 'He was poisoned by his children and stabbed by his wife.'

'Good,' said Isabella. 'He looks like he deserved it.' She laughed; a porcelain tinkle of a laugh, which earned an angry glare from a museum custodian.

The centre of the gallery was dominated by a life-sized wax sculpture of Good Prince Eugene, sitting atop his stallion, Maximus. The figure had been on display for nearly seventy years and the wax head was so badly melted that the face was almost unrecognisable as that of a human. The fingers had grown brittle and snapped off, and the sawdust stuffing of the horse collected in piles on the floor, like mounds of curiously pale horse dung. The custodians of the museum were obliged to sweep this from the gallery three times a day, before re-stuffing the horse every night.

Osbert remembered Good Prince Eugene from the picture books his father had read to him. The Prince was a brave soldier, who had fought many great battles to free the people of Schwartzgarten from the evil rule of Emeté Talbor. But like all good men, once Good Prince Eugene seized power, he became fat and lazy. He had to ride around the city on a mechanical horse which ran on special rails set into the cobbled streets because his trusty stallion had died, buckling under his master's immense weight. When Prince Eugene died, he had reached such an enormous size that the bodies of his ancestors had to be removed from the family vault in the Schwartzgarten cemetery to make room for the fat Prince to be interred.

'Was Emeté Talbor a very evil man?' asked Isabella, a ghoulish tremor in her voice.

'Yes,' said Osbert. 'He was. Nobody knows how many people he killed. He particularly liked chopping his enemies' heads off with a guillotine.'

'How bloodthirsty,' gasped Isabella, secretly wishing that there were photographs of the guillotine in action.

The cracked helmet, the shattered sword and the jewelled gauntlets that Prince Eugene had used in battle were displayed in a glass cabinet. Everything Osbert had read in the history books was there before him in the display case.

Isabella peered through the glass and read from a neatly-typed description pinned inside the cabinet.

'Emeté Talbor's dark heart was plucked from the cavity of his chest, and was burnt in a flaming brazier outside the city walls. The following year, the event was commemorated by the Guild of Jewellers, who carved a replica of the heart from a solid block of Carpathian jet, encrusted with two hundred and forty-one tiny diamonds, one for every month of Emeté Talbor's reign of terror.'

Osbert walked Isabella back to the Myops' pastry

shop, then headed for home along the banks of the River Schwartz. But his journey was interrupted by an unexpected and alarming sight; gathered on the Princess Euphenia Bridge were a group of police constables and the Inspector of Police. The Inspector was barking orders at a further two constables, who were carefully negotiating the waters of the River Schwartz in a tiny rowing boat.

'Just reach in and get it,' bawled the Inspector. 'Have I got to do everything myself?' At his side, Massimo yawned and whined impatiently.

Osbert peered over the bridge and was mortified to discover the cause of the excitement. A wooden box had become lodged between two rocks, and one of the police constables was bravely leaning out of the boat, attempting to secure the box with a fishing net. It was not just any box, but Osbert's box of evidence.

'What do you think it is, Inspector?' shouted the Constable.

'Think I'm a mind reader, do you?' shouted back the Inspector. 'All I'm saying is this – and I'm standing by it – that box looks interesting.'

The Constable took another swipe with the net. Osbert watched and held his breath. If the box was rescued, he was certain his plan was at an end. He would be discovered.

Fortunately for Osbert, as he stood contemplating his next move, the police boat was capsized by the relentless flow of the River Schwartz and the police constables were forced to swim to shore. Furthermore, the box became dislodged from the rocks, smashed open in the surging water and was carried towards the forest as Osbert had originally intended. Breathing a sigh of relief, Osbert patted Massimo and continued on his way.

But this was not the end of the box. Osbert's heart would have lurched in his chest had he realised that Mr Rudulfus was standing downstream on the banks of the River Schwartz, preparing to abduct forest animals to be mounted for his collection of taxidermy. As Rudulfus stooped to chloroform an unfortunate river rat, Osbert's box of evidence washed up at his very feet.

CHAPTER TWELVE

A FAIR WAS mounted every year to commemorate the defeat of Emeté Talbor, which in time became a large street market, which had in turn become a great festival: the Festival of Prince Eugene.

But with two weeks to go before the Festival, all was not well. The city was sick at heart.

WHO WILL DIE NEXT? demanded a headline in *The Informant*.

Are we safe in our beds? inquired an editorial in *The Schwartzgarten Daily Examiner*.

The citizens of Schwartzgarten were consumed with fear. They gathered in vast numbers outside the Governor's Palace, anxious for reassurance that they would not all be murdered by the Slayer. A platform had been erected, and the Inspector of Police mounted the steps. He called out across the crowded square.

'Citizens of Schwartzgarten!' he began.

'Speak up!' screamed a woman in the crowd.

The Inspector strained his eyes to pick out the woman. The face was unmistakable, almost more terrifying than the Schwartzgarten Slayer. It was the Inspector's wife.

'Darling?' he called.

'Don't you darling me!' bawled the woman. 'What are you going to do about the Schwartzgarten Slayer, bonehead?'

There was loud laughter from the crowd.

'I'm doing the best I can,' cried the Inspector.

'Well, your best isn't good enough, is it?' called his wife. 'If you didn't have pudding for brains, maybe you'd have the Slayer locked up behind bars where he belongs, not running amok out here murdering innocent citizens.'

'The city is crawling with my very best men,' insisted the Inspector.

'Crawling, that's the word,' answered his wife. 'Can't do anything at the proper speed.'

'If you don't shut up, I'll have you arrested!' screamed the Inspector.

'I'd like to see the constable that would try it!' shrieked his wife. 'If they're no match for the Slayer, then they're no match for me!'

The Inspector raised his hands to silence the crowd.

'Citizens,' he pleaded. 'Citizens, please! The streets are patrolled day and night, even our sewers are patrolled!'

'Best place for a big stink like you!' cackled his wife.

The Inspector's moustache twitched and bristled with anger.

'I tell you this much,' he vowed. 'Before the Festival of Prince Eugene I'll have the Schwartzgarten Slayer under lock and key.'

Osbert, who had been watching events with interest, felt an exquisite pang of sympathy for the Inspector, but that could not be helped. As Nanny sometimes said, 'If you pity the pig, you miss out on the bacon.'

In the week preceding the Festival, the shops which lined Edvardplatz filled their windows with elaborately decorated displays. Most impressive of all were the premises of the chocolate maker, M. Kalvitas, who piled his windows high with precarious towers of almond nougat and brittle slabs of chocolate praline. There were dark chocolate cherubs, brushed with edible gold leaf, with terrifying chocolate gargoyles perched on their shoulders, and a milk chocolate head that had been moulded from a cast of Emeté Talbor's death mask.

One bitterly cold evening three days before the Festival, wrapped in a black coat and moth-eaten fur hat, Nanny took Osbert to M. Kalvitas's to buy salted caramels.

'A treat for the Festival,' she cackled.

It was a marvellous shop to behold. The upper shelves bulged under the weight of chocolate boxes of every shape and colour, while the lower shelves were home to a peculiar menagerie of chocolate rats, ravens and winged demons. Behind the counter there were neat stacks of brightly coloured macaroons tied with bows of red ribbon, tins of cocoa, glass jars of crystallised ginger, gold and silver sugared almonds and liquorice diabolos. The warm scent of cocoa was everywhere, made more pungent by the steaming glasses of molten hot chocolate that were dispensed from a glittering golden chocolate pot, engraved with the likeness of Good Prince Eugene.

'Hello, Osbert,' said Isabella, who sat in a corner of the shop with her mother. She sipped from a glass of hot chocolate, topped with peaks of whipped cream and a thick sprinkling of chocolate vermicelli.

'Little Osbert,' said Mrs Myop, who was wrapped snugly in an elegant mink coat and a large fur hat. 'What a surprise. Have you heard the wonderful news?'

'Has something happened?' asked Osbert, suddenly uneasy.

'I should say it has,' said Mrs Myop, glowing with pride. 'We've come to buy Isabella a new dress. Our darling is to be Princess of the Festival.'

Isabella smiled, her upper lip smeared with cream and melted chocolate. She reached inside her purse and pulled out three tickets.

'For the carnival tent,' said Isabella. 'You can bring your mother and father and watch me take my throne as Princess of the Festival.'

'Remember you were only given *twenty* tickets,' cautioned Mrs Myop, who knew that tickets to the carnival tent were hard to come by and did not want them wasted on the impoverished Brinkhoff family.

'May I have a fourth ticket?' asked Osbert. 'For Nanny,' he explained, not wishing to be thought of as greedy.

Isabella smiled and produced a fourth ticket. Mrs Myop slurped her hot chocolate impatiently.

'Look,' said Isabella, holding out a box.

Inside was the most expensive chocolate confection that M. Kalvitas had to offer: a perfect tinplate replica of Good Prince Eugene's imperial carriage, with moving tin wheels and a clockwork mechanism. Inside, wrapped in foil, was a dark chocolate effigy of the prince, stuffed from head to toe with rich almond marzipan. It was traditional for children fortunate enough to be presented with such a model to bite off the head of the prince and send the clockwork carriage careering across their bedroom floors with the decapitated marzipan and chocolate corpse rattling around inside.

But it was another clockwork figure that was attracting Osbert's attention. In the centre of the shop, on a table stacked with Pfefferberg's Nougat Marshmallows, was a perfect scale model of the Star Box.

The Star Box had been used for many years, to represent the death-by-burning of Emeté Talbor's second-in-command, General Akibus. Akibus was a cruel man, known to the people of Schwartzgarten as the Dark Count. Under the orders of Good Prince Eugene, and to purge the city of darkness, Akibus had been locked inside a wooden box filled with gunpowder. But after the box had erupted, there were no remains of the man to be seen; it was as though the Dark Count had melted into the night.

Every year, at the grand finale of the Festival, Mr Rudulfus would take the part of Akibus, climbing into the Star Box with the raven mask once worn by the Vigils, Emeté Talbor's most loyal foot soldiers. Mr Rudulfus would be handcuffed inside the box, which had been painted with stars and constellations, with barely seconds to escape before a burning fuse set fire to an explosive charge of gunpowder.

Children pushed past to take huge handfuls of the Pfefferberg marshmallows, but Osbert stood transfixed. Inside the miniature Star Box, a tiny clockwork figure of Mr Rudulfus, his head covered by the long-beaked raven mask, struggled and wriggled as if trying to escape.

'He's quite lost to the world,' said Mrs Myop, as Nanny prodded Osbert, clutching her bag of caramels.

Isabella gazed at the squirming clockwork figure of Mr Rudulfus. 'Wouldn't it be awful,' she whispered with a smile, 'if somebody tampered with the mechanism of the handcuffs, and Mr Rudulfus *wasn't* able to escape from the Star Box?'

It was as though Isabella had the power to read Osbert's thoughts. He had spent many days devising a plan for Mr Rudulfus to be pecked to death by ravens, but there was something eminently satisfying about the prospect of a more explosive end to the man...

'It's time to go back to the Old Town,' said Nanny.

'Perhaps this will bring him round,' said Mrs Myop, opening her purse and taking out a red foil-wrapped Pfefferberg marshmallow. 'With your father and mother so terribly poor, I suppose you hardly ever see chocolate.'

'Thank you,' said Osbert, taking the marshmallow.

'Goodbye, Osbert,' said Isabella, smiling and biting the head off Prince Eugene.

As Nanny pulled the door closed behind them, Osbert unwrapped the foil of the Pfefferberg marshmallow and took a bite into the crisp chocolate shell, his teeth sinking into the creamy mallow filling and the chewy layer of nougat. There was much to occupy his mind.

<hr>

The next morning, as Osbert walked across Edvardplatz on his way to visit Isabella, a sudden darkening of the sky heralded the arrival of Mr Rudulfus. He had an alarming habit of disappearing and reappearing, as if by magic.

'Cursed creatures!' he mumbled, rounding a corner as the dense fog of ravens circled above his head. He held in his hand a large leather case.

'I don't know what's wrong with the man,' whispered

a market trader to his customer. 'He's been walking round and round all morning. As if he's looking for something.'

'Or else he's gone mad,' suggested the customer.

Mr Rudulfus gazed around him and his glance seemed to fall on Osbert, who stepped back behind the market stall, not wishing to be seen.

Mr Rudulfus hurried from the square, followed by Osbert at a discreet distance. He scuttled along Marshal Podovsky Street, through the gates into the large courtyard in front of the Schwartzgarten Museum, finally escaping the ravens, which perched impatiently on the gates, awaiting the re-emergence of their prey.

The museum was an impressive building, flanked by a row of elegant Corinthian columns, with bas-relief carvings of great moments in Schwartzgarten's history decorating each and every stone wall. In the centre of the courtyard stood a copper statue of Marshal Berghopf, his hair white with pigeon droppings.

Osbert paid his admission and walked into the museum's dark entrance vestibule. He arrived in time to see Mr Rudulfus climbing the narrow marble staircase at the farthest corner of the entrance hall. Osbert followed cautiously, tracking his former teacher as the man climbed the steps to the Gallery of Oddities.

As Osbert reached the top of the stairs he was alarmed to find Mr Rudulfus waiting for him. Osbert took a step backwards, almost tumbling back down the staircase.

'Are you following me, boy?' demanded Mr Rudulfus.

'No, sir,' gasped Osbert.

Mr Rudulfus took a step forward. 'Osbert Brinkhoff, isn't it?'

'No,' stammered Osbert. 'My name is…my name is Milo Mylinsky.'

Mr Rudulfus gave a knowing smile and walked away quickly across the marble floor, disappearing through a door marked: *GALLERY OF ODDITIES. CUSTODIAN'S OFFICE.*

Loud voices could soon be heard from inside.

'This is not good enough,' came the unmistakable voice of Mr Rudulfus.

'Everything is in order,' came a second, older voice. 'We have followed your plans to the letter, Mr Rudulfus.'

Osbert waited outside the door, but the argument soon dropped in volume and he could make out nothing but an indistinct mumble. He turned his attention to the Gallery of Oddities, which housed an unusual assortment of objects that had no place in the other galleries of the museum. Osbert was intrigued by an ingenious coin-in-the-slot automaton of the large Indian elephant that had trampled to death the brave but unfortunate Marshal Borgburg as he made his victory parade through the city of Schwartzgarten on his return from battle, bringing the elephant home as a souvenir from an enemy zoo. Osbert put a curseling in the slot and watched as the mechanism sprang into life. A tiny set of bellows inside the body of the elephant created the roar of the mighty beast, and the creature's feet rose and fell, as though trampling to death the carved wooden figure of the unhappy marshal.

Suddenly, the door of the office opened and an elderly museum custodian shuffled out from inside. He was small, with a grey moustache and beard and a beetroot-red complexion. In his hands he clutched a pile of papers. There was no sign of Mr Rudulfus.

'What are you doing?' demanded the custodian. 'Loitering?'

'I wasn't loitering,' replied Osbert politely.

'Don't contradict,' spat the custodian. He tapped at the blue enamel badge he wore on the lapel of his jacket. 'I'm the custodian,' he said. 'What I say goes.' He shook his head, miserably. 'You're as bad as that Rudulfus.' He jerked his head back in the direction of the office. 'Questioning everything I tell him. Comes in here like he owns the place.'

'But why?' asked Osbert.

'I'll tell you why,' said the custodian, 'but don't come too close. Children's germs are death to a man as old as me.' Osbert kept his distance and waited patiently for the custodian's explanation. 'That Star Box for the Festival of Prince Eugene, it's going to be stored in the Gallery of Oddities for safe keeping.'

This was news indeed, and Osbert could hardly prevent a smile from flickering across his face.

'On and on about that box,' continued the custodian.

'What does he know about the Star Box that I don't? Well, what?'

'I don't know,' replied Osbert.

'Nothing,' said the custodian, bitterly. 'But it's the Star Box this, and the Star Box that. Listening to him talk you'd think he'd designed that damned Star Box himself. Well, he didn't.'

'No,' said Osbert.

'No,' said the custodian. 'He thinks he knows so much, but he knows nothing. *Nothing.*'

'What do you mean?' asked Osbert.

'What I mean is this,' said the man, lowering his voice to a rattling whisper. 'The Gallery of Oddities isn't as safe and secure as Rudulfus thinks.' He pulled a map from the pile of papers he carried. 'He hasn't seen this.'

'What is it?' asked Osbert.

'A map of the gallery,' said the custodian, 'and marked on that map is a secret passage.'

Osbert could barely believe his good fortune.

'It would turn Rudulfus's hair as white as mine if he knew of that passage,' the custodian went on. 'But he won't know, because I won't tell him. I'll just clutch on tight to this map and I won't breathe a word. Now don't come so close. What did I say about germs?'

With that he waved the pile of papers and shuffled away, mumbling to himself. As he did so, the map slid out from his bundle of papers and dropped to the floor. But the custodian did not notice and carried on walking. Osbert waited until the man had vanished from sight, then stooped to pick up the fallen map. He unfolded the paper to reveal a plan of the Gallery of Oddities, more than a hundred years old. Marked clearly on the map was a concealed passageway leading into the gallery.

Osbert smiled. He folded the map carefully, slipped it inside his pocket and walked quickly from the museum.

———•—•———

The next day the Star Box was taken out of storage and wheeled to the Gallery of Oddities, where it was examined carefully by Mr Rudulfus. When he was quite convinced that it had not been tampered with, responsibility for protecting the Star Box was passed to the Inspector of Police. The custodian of the gallery was nowhere to be seen.

The gallery door was locked and bolted, and two armed guards stood outside. The Inspector paced excitedly, his moustache quivering with satisfaction.

'The Schwartzgarten Slayer won't be getting in there, not with two guards standing sentry,' he declared.

'The room is quite impregnable,' agreed Mr Rudulfus, smiling oddly. 'No second door, no windows. Just solid stone walls.'

That night, Osbert cautiously approached the museum, finding his way easily in the sharp, blue moonlight. Carved into a side wall of the building was an elaborate stone frieze, charting Emperor Xavier's life from infancy to tyranny. The frieze began with Xavier's coronation at the tender age of five, and illustrated all of his famous and bloody battles, depicted in gruesome detail. Osbert followed the frieze to the back of the museum, where few citizens of the city ever set foot and far from the prying eyes of the police. He was searching for the entrance to the secret passage. The final panel of the frieze showed a decrepit and bearded Emperor Xavier seated at his throne, and at his feet the hunched form of a lion, symbolising Xavier's dominion over his enemies.

It was the lion that was attracting Osbert's attention. According to the plans the custodian had dropped, this was the panel that covered the entrance to the passageway, and had clearly been marked with the word *Leo*, the Latin for lion.

Osbert made certain that no one was watching him, and then pressed the carved beast with both hands. But nothing happened. Wiping the lenses of his spectacles, Osbert stared hard at the surface of the stone beast. There were no obvious handles, no recesses that might have concealed a lever. But as Osbert passed his hands over the carving he noticed that the left eye of the lion had a different texture to that of the right. The left eye was smoother to the touch, colder somehow. The eye was forged from metal.

Osbert smiled. He pressed the eye, which stiffly

receded into the wall. With a groan and creak of ancient metal, the stone panel slid upwards, revealing the pitch-black passageway beyond. Osbert switched on his pocket torch and took a step inside the chamber. On the wall to his left was a rusted lever, swathed in cobwebs, which was obviously used to close the secret panel. Only by tugging with both arms was Osbert able to move the lever, covering his hands with flakes of bright orange rust. The panel slid back into place.

Shining his torch in front of him, Osbert made his way along the dusty floor, pulling aside veils of cobwebs and dodging the fat black rats that shuttled along the hidden passageway. A narrow stone staircase, as smooth as the day it was hewn many hundreds of years before, led up inside the wall of the museum. Osbert slowly made his way from step to step. At the top of the staircase, on a small landing, a niche had been carved into the dark grey stone. Set into the niche was another lever, almost shrouded from view by cobwebs. Osbert reached inside and pulled. As the lever gave way, a nest of spiderlings dropped onto his outstretched fingers. He gasped and withdrew his hand, waving his arm desperately as the tiny black creatures surged along the sleeve of his jacket. He was so distracted that he had not noticed the door had silently opened, revealing the Gallery of Oddities beyond. He shone his torch inside, and the beam came to rest on the brightly painted Star Box.

And now, thought Osbert, climbing into the silent and deserted gallery, *now to tamper with the mechanism.*

As Osbert placed his hands against the side of the Star Box he was unaware that he was being watched. The eyes of Marshal Borgburg's painting followed Osbert's every move.

———

It was the afternoon before the Festival of Prince Eugene and the cafés and taverns were full to overflowing with the Guildsmen of the city who, every year, would drink late into the night.

Mr Rudulfus rode in the back of a taxicab to the Bank of Muller, Baum and Spink, watching with irritation as the driver weaved in and out of the crowds of revellers.

Mr Spink and Mr Baum had given instructions that the doors of the bank should be closed at five o'clock precisely, so their staff would be able to return home to enjoy the festivities. The cashiers were therefore saddened to discover Mr Rudulfus stepping from his taxicab at five minutes to the hour of five. He entered the bank and strode purposefully across the chequered floor.

'I wish to withdraw money from The Institute's account,' he demanded, without a smile or a pleasant word to mark the festive occasion.

'How much money do you wish to withdraw, sir?' asked the cashier, unable to stop his hands from trembling.

Mr Rudulfus wrote the sum on a slip of paper and pushed it across the counter.

The cashier stared in disbelief at the paper. 'I will call for Mr Spink at once.'

Mr Spink was also staggered by Mr Rudulfus's request, and wondered if the man had simply forgotten to stop adding noughts at the end of the figure.

'Fifty thousand imperial crowns?' asked Mr Spink, smiling nervously. 'Is that quite correct?'

'For a new security mechanism to be installed at The Institute,' explained Mr Rudulfus. 'To repel the Schwartzgarten Slayer. What is money, if it won't protect the life of our beloved Principal?'

As Mr Rudulfus had confidently predicted, Mr Spink did not dare to question his word. It was a Friday night, and the Principal would not discover that the money had been withdrawn until the following Monday, by which time it would be too late.

In accordance with tradition, the children of Schwartzgarten had been sent to bed early, the windows shuttered, locked in their bedrooms with a bag of purple 'sugared noses'. Emeté Talbor had despised children, and was notorious for slicing off the noses of disagreeable infants with the tip of his ceremonial silver sword. The sugared noses were a grim reminder of darker days. Talbor's dislike for children was so great that he had drowned all fifteen of his own babies in a bathtub, so that they could never grow up to challenge his iron grip on the city of Schwartzgarten.

By the light of flaming torches, the guildsmen and aldermen processed slowly towards the Old Town, weaving through the streets and alleys on their journey to the cemetery. Isabella, as Princess of the Festival, followed behind with her retinue. And at a distance came Osbert, slinking through the shadows.

He watched as the party arrived at Emeté Talbor's grand vault in the Schwartzgarten Municipal Cemetery and the tomb was opened. The cobwebs were gently pulled away from Talbor's skeletal remains and the grisly corpse was placed upright in a large golden throne.

'Hello, Isabella,' said Osbert, seeming to materialise out of thin air.

Isabella jumped. 'What are you doing here?' she asked. 'Shouldn't you be locked up at home?'

'Nanny doesn't believe in locking children up,' said Osbert. 'And besides,' he added with a smile, 'I wanted to see you.'

'Bow before me, loyal subject,' said Isabella, returning the smile.

Osbert bowed.

'Chocolate caramel?' asked Isabella, holding out a bag.

'What about the sugared noses?' asked Osbert.

'I ate them,' said Isabella. 'I can do anything. I'm Princess of the Festival.'

Osbert waited with Isabella until a ceremonial legion of a hundred men, dressed in the uniforms of Emeté Talbor's Imperial Army, gathered in the cemetery to stand guard over the corpse of the tyrant ruler.

'I'll see you tomorrow,' said Osbert. 'I have a feeling it's going to be the most explosive Festival the city has ever seen.'

CHAPTER THIRTEEN

❖

THE MORNING of the Festival was one of the coldest Schwartzgarten had ever known, and ribbons of low-lying mist swirled and eddied along the cobbled streets. At daybreak, singing battle songs, the legion of soldiers carried the golden throne aloft, conveying their decomposing leader across the Princess Euphenia Bridge, towards Edvardplatz.

In the New Town, a second procession had begun, starting at the gates of the Governor's Palace. A painted effigy of Good Prince Eugene was carried between the bustling market stalls of Edvardplatz, surrounded by guildsmen wielding painted white branches to symbolise the Prince's goodness. At twelve noon, as the clock tower struck the hour, the two armies converged. With a terrifying blast of military horns, the two groups re-enacted the great battle as Isabella watched from a platform at the edge of the square.

It was a long battle and took the greater part of the

day to act out, but by nightfall, as the crowds massed on Edvardplatz, the fighting was almost at an end. The crisp, icy air was rich with the smell of hot spiced apple schnapps and warm gingerbread. Stallholders sold large wedges of fruitcake, fried in butter and dusted with cinnamon and confectioner's sugar. There were apple dumplings with plum sauce, pancakes with warm vanilla syrup and hot caramelised filberts.

Osbert had been told to keep a close watch on Nanny, in case the lure of spiced apple schnapps proved too strong for her. Mrs Brinkhoff had remained at home with Mr Brinkhoff, tending to her husband until he felt strong enough to be wheeled out to the carnival tent for the evening's celebrations.

'Oh, the temptations of the bottle!' moaned Nanny, eyeing the neatly-lined bottles of schnapps on a market stall.

Osbert bought Nanny a large red helium balloon to distract her from drink, as they pushed through the crowds on Edvardplatz, making their way towards the mechanical carousel, The Horsemen Of The Apocalypse. Osbert had always loved the carousel, with its beautifully carved wooden stallions: the white horse for war, the red horse for slaughter, the black horse for famine and the pale horse for death. Osbert sat on the red horse. 'Death Comes A-Waltzing' played mournfully on the carousel organ as the roundabout whirred and creaked into life.

Sitting on top of the painted wooden horse afforded an excellent view over Edvardplatz. Osbert could observe the surging masses as they thronged around the stalls and sideshows which surrounded the carnival tent. The tent itself was very large, occupying a good quarter of Edvardplatz. It was constructed of black and white striped canvas, and decorated with skulls and devils carved from wood and painted in gold. Alongside the carnival tent, between the stand for boiled beef and pickles and the stall of the silhouette cutter, a small green tent was attracting a lot of business. Above the tent was a brightly painted sign: *Madame Irina, Mystic.*

Osbert watched with interest as Mr Rudulfus emerged furtively from the carnival tent and scurried towards the mystic's booth, cowering from the ravens which had been attracted by the rich scraps of food littering the cobbles of Edvardplatz. Osbert wondered if Madame Irina could predict the events that were about to unfold that evening. He doubted that she could.

———•———

Mr Rudulfus did not even have time to sit down before Madame Irina offered a prediction.

'Your end will be an untimely one,' said the mystic, who had been gripped by the stories in *The Informant*, and knew full well that the teachers at The Institute were being picked off, one by one.

'And will my death have something to do with ravens?' inquired Mr Rudulfus.

'It might do,' replied Madame Irina, vaguely. 'Yes,' she continued. 'I see ravens. Definitely ravens.'

'We shall see,' said Mr Rudulfus, with a smile that chilled the mystic's heart. 'We shall see.'

He returned to the carnival tent, nodding to the Inspector of Police as he walked swiftly past the rows of seats and up onto the stage.

'I do not want to be disturbed,' said Mr Rudulfus.

He flicked a switch and was slowly lowered through the trap door, disappearing from sight.

—■—

Night had fallen, and Edvardplatz was illuminated by a ring of flaming braziers. The rival armies were enacting the final battle between Good Prince Eugene and Emeté Talbor.

The drums beat slowly, the horns were sounded and the army of Emeté Talbor sang a dirge as the throne of the Emperor sank to the ground.

'The tyrant is dead!' came the cry. 'Long live Good Prince Eugene!'

'Here she comes,' said Nanny as Isabella appeared from the crowd of soldiers, dressed in an ermine-lined cloak and white leather gloves.

Osbert watched in awe.

'Pluck out the heart, the heart that enslaved us!' chanted the soldiers.

Isabella approached the throne and pulled up her sleeve. The sickly-sweet stench of Emeté Talbor's corpse was almost unbearable, so she breathed through her mouth as she reached into his ribcage to extract the jet heart.

'The heart of the tyrant!' she shouted, holding the jewelled stone aloft.

There were loud cheers from the crowd as Talbor's corpse was pulled from the throne and his rotting bones were swung into a ceremonial coffin, to be carried back to the cemetery. A crown was lowered onto Isabella's head. She took her place on the throne, which was hoisted high by eight soldiers, who weaved their way through the stalls and sideshows as they began a circuitous and ceremonial route to the carnival tent where the evening's entertainment would be held.

Osbert waited expectantly with Nanny for the audience to be admitted. The entrance was flanked on either side by large distorting mirrors. Nanny laughed at her reflection; she looked as thin as she had been the fateful day Marshal Potemkin had been poisoned. Osbert on the other hand appeared twice his natural height, and oddly sinister. So sinister in fact, he was convinced that people would point and scream, 'There he is! *There's* the Schwartzgarten Slayer!'

But of course, it was just his distorted reflection.

'Look,' cried Nanny, pointing into the distance. There, rattling over the cobbles, came Mr Brinkhoff in his invalid chair, pushed by Mrs Brinkhoff.

'You came,' said Osbert, delighted.

'I couldn't miss the Festival,' laughed Mr Brinkhoff, as Mrs Brinkhoff tucked a blanket around his legs.

'I told him he should stay in the warm, but he wouldn't hear of it,' said Mrs Brinkhoff, smiling.

Their happiness was shattered by a loud motor horn as a sleek black limousine, gleaming with wax polish, rolled onto the cobbles and ground to a halt. The driver's door opened and the Porter appeared, dressed in a buttoned jacket, leather gauntlets and peaked cap. He opened the passenger door and the Principal emerged from within, leaning heavily on his Malacca cane as he raised himself to his full height. It seemed to Osbert as though the man had grown by at least twelve inches since their last encounter at The Institute. The crowd fell silent. As the Principal passed Osbert, blithely unaware that he was within inches of the Schwartzgarten Slayer, Mr Brinkhoff let out an involuntary gasp. The Principal stopped in his tracks and swung round, drinking in the huddled family cowering before him.

'Brinkhoff,' said the Principal. It was not Osbert he was addressing, but his father. 'In an invalid chair, I see.' He smiled. 'Not enough sense in that withered brain of yours to keep you upright any more?'

'There's nothing wrong with his brain,' said Osbert, and Mrs Brinkhoff seized his coat sleeve in alarm.

'And little Osbert Brinkhoff,' continued the Principal, a thin wisp of breath escaping from his lips and condensing in the freezing air. 'Still haven't learned any manners, I see.' He smiled once more; his lips pulled back to reveal receding and bloodied gums. 'I hope you enjoy your evening. There must be precious little to keep you amused in your wretched lives.' And with that he turned on his heel and strode off towards the tent.

Mr Brinkhoff attempted a smile, but his hands shook.

'A glass of spiced rye beer will sort you out,' said Mrs Brinkhoff, gently squeezing her husband's shoulder.

The accordion player from the Emperor Xavier Hotel had been hired for the evening, and played traditional folk songs as the audience entered the tent. The central dome of stretched canvas was supported by twelve red wooden struts, and each strut was in turn supported by a wooden pillar, set with tiny mirrors and carved to represent the allegorical story of Death pursuing Beauty. Filigree lanterns hung from the ceiling, casting flickering skeletal faces across the floor.

At the far end of the tent sat the burghers of Schwartzgarten: the guildsmen and aldermen, drinking from tankards of hot rye beer, served by women in traditional Schwartzgarten costume. Among their number sat the Principal, sipping from a glass of schnapps at the side of the stage, a look of malevolent satisfaction etched on his face.

The audience took their seats. Osbert sat with Nanny, and Mrs Brinkhoff sat beside Mr Brinkhoff, holding a tankard of spiced rye beer to his lips. Mr Brinkhoff's hands were still trembling from his encounter with the Principal.

'All right, men,' said the Inspector of Police in a hushed voice to a small army of police constables, 'if you see anything suspicious, I want to be the first to know about it. Is that clear?'

A trumpet sounded, and Isabella entered, carried aloft on Emeté Talbor's golden throne. As the audience applauded, she waved to her loyal subjects and reached down to take a chocolate from the box she had concealed beside her on the throne. Deliberating over whether to take a chocolate caramel or a lingonberry cream, she discovered a less palatable sweetmeat beneath the lid of the chocolate box: one of Emeté Talbor's skeletal fingers had snapped off at the knuckle, and had not been carried back to the tomb. She picked up the grisly object and flung it from the throne, laughing as it dropped with a splash into the spiced rye beer of an elderly alderman.

The throne was lowered into its final position at the back of the tent, giving Isabella an excellent vantage point for the evening's entertainments. Osbert, who sat two rows in front of Isabella, was relieved to find that his friend would be safely out of harm's way.

A hissing gas lamp illuminated the stage and the orchestra struck up as the Master of Ceremonies fought his way through the curtains.

'Ladies and gentlemen,' he announced, bowing elaborately. 'I bid you welcome.'

The man wore a long black velvet cape, his bald head covered by a neatly oiled wig, which slipped down his forehead whenever he raised his eyebrows.

'For your delectation and enjoyment on this day, the Festival of Prince Eugene, we shall bring you music, laughter, high drama, certain thrills, unexpected chills, a cornucopia of entertainment so exotic and spectacular that it will take you until next Festival night for your hearts and minds to recover.' He bowed again as the audience applauded enthusiastically.

Osbert sat upright and expectant in his seat as the Master of Ceremonies silenced the audience with a wave of his hands. 'But first, ladies and gentlemen, may I present to you the distinguished Deputy Principal of The Institute, Mr Aristotle Rudulfus…'

On cue, Mr Rudulfus stepped onto the stage. He was dressed for the occasion in a black suit with a starched wing collar and an immaculately knotted violet necktie. He wore black leather gloves and carried the long-beaked raven mask under his arm. The Principal applauded loudly, and the audience followed his example, through fear rather than enthusiasm.

Mr Rudulfus grimaced as he faced the audience, squinting in the bright lamplight. Through his one good eye he could just make out the figure of Osbert Brinkhoff. He smiled to himself, quite certain that Osbert would not move from his seat until the Star Box appeared on stage. He made a slight bow of his head. 'May tonight be full of surprises and intrigues.'

There was a whirring of motors and Mr Rudulfus gave another bow as he slowly disappeared through the trap door in the stage.

'Bring on the first act,' croaked the Master of Ceremonies, and his assistant shoved three terrified singers onto the stage. 'The Terpsichore Triplets,' he announced, 'who will sing "The Ballad of Good Prince Eugene".'

Nanny sat back in her seat and grinned, sipping schnapps from a hip flask she had concealed inside her coat. 'Now sing up,' she gurgled. 'Sing up!'

Osbert found it amusing to watch Nanny's reactions to the acts. The Terpsichore Triplets were so anxious at the sight of the Principal that they seemed incapable of singing in tune. Impatiently, Nanny hurled a dry cinnamon bun at the head of the tallest triplet, but even this did not improve their performance and they were booed from the stage.

Nanny cooed and chuckled as a performing monkey was ushered out from behind the curtains. But the ape was so bored that his keeper had to prod him with a stick to keep him awake.

'Bite him!' urged Nanny, who always had sympathy for caged creatures. 'Scratch him! Go for the eyes!'

The monkey seemed to share Nanny's opinion, and after one particularly violent prod turned on his keeper, scratching wildly as he chased the man from the stage.

'That's right!' cackled Nanny. 'You teach him a lesson!'

'And now,' cried the Master of Ceremonies, attempting to drown out the shrieking monkey and the blood-curdling howls of his unfortunate keeper, 'the Amazing Adolpho!'

Adolpho was a sword swallower, and was anything but amazing. Owing to an inflammation of the throat, he could only swallow spoons and even this he did with tears in his eyes.

Nanny stamped her feet impatiently as act after act failed to impress her. It was a long evening, especially for Osbert, who patiently awaited the spectacular climax to the festivities.

The 'thrills' that had been promised failed to materialise and the 'chills' were not chilling. Isabella continued to watch with regal dispassion from her throne, drinking peppermint cordial loudly through a straw. She was suddenly aware of a small woman in a hat and silver fox-fur stole leaning towards her.

'I expect you would like more chocolates,' said the woman with a low purr.

Isabella smiled down at the woman and nodded hungrily. 'I like lingonberry creams the most,' she said.

'If you follow me, you can have as many lingonberry

creams as your heart desires,' said the woman.

Isabella went willingly and greedily and Osbert watched curiously as the woman led his friend away. A number of ravens had gathered at the entrance to the carnival tent, pecking at fallen scraps of food. One of the birds squawked loudly and Osbert watched in horror as the woman in the fox-fur stole jerked her head in alarm. Osbert caught sight of her face; the right eye was blind and milky.

Making sure that Nanny and his mother and father were not looking, Osbert slipped from his seat and followed Isabella and the woman as they walked out onto Edvardplatz, hurrying off towards a silent street beyond the cobbled square. They stopped outside the shuttered windows of a small abandoned shop.

'Where are the chocolates?' asked Isabella, who had grown bored of walking.

'Just inside this door,' said the woman, leading the girl inside the empty shop.

Osbert watched through a crack in the shutters.

'But I can't *see* any chocolates,' said Isabella impatiently. 'There's nothing here.'

Before she could utter another word, a cotton pad soaked in chloroform had been clamped over her nose and mouth. Isabella fought for air, but there was nothing but chloroform to inhale. She slumped into the woman's arms, and was carefully lowered to the floor. The woman removed her hat and her fox-fur, finally revealing the grinning face of Mr Rudulfus. Osbert felt his stomach lurch with fear.

Mr Rudulfus lifted a picture from the wall and pressed a hidden switch. A panel at the back of the shop slid open, leading to a hidden passageway beyond. He took a torch from his pocket and dragged Isabella through the secret doorway, the wall sliding back into position behind them.

Osbert entered the shop and pressed his ear against the wall, waiting until the sound of footsteps had receded into the distance. He was almost deafened by the thumping of his own heart. Following Mr Rudulfus's example, he pressed the hidden switch and the secret panel slid away as before. He did not have a torch and could only find his way in the darkness by running his hands along the cold stone wall of the passageway, which began to descend sharply. He guessed correctly that he was passing beneath Edvardplatz.

It took Osbert many minutes to reach the end of the tunnel, which was illuminated dimly by flickering lamplight. An iron ladder had been set in the wall, and he cautiously climbed the rungs, peering up into the chamber above. He almost gasped in horror; there was Mr Rudulfus, standing on a small stepladder, fastening Isabella inside the Star Box. There was a muffled round of applause, and Osbert realised at once that the chamber was beneath the stage of the carnival tent.

'What's happening?' moaned Isabella, finally recovering from the chloroform. Her head throbbed and her mouth felt sticky. 'Where am I?'

'So, you are awake,' said Mr Rudulfus. 'Excellent. It would have been disappointing had you missed this.'

'What are you doing?' Isabella demanded.

Mr Rudulfus nodded. 'It is quite right that you should ask that question,' he replied. 'An inquisitive mind. I have decided that the Star Box is too dangerous, and that you should take my place instead.'

'But why?' asked Isabella.

'The answer is quite simple,' said Mr Rudulfus, dressing Isabella in his patent leather shoes and black gloves as she lay inside the Star Box. 'Because the Schwartzgarten Slayer is intending to kill me, and I would prefer it if he killed you instead.' Isabella squirmed in the box, struggling to escape. But it was no use, she was firmly held in position. 'Fortunately we are the same height, Isabella. Good fortune for me, but a misfortune for you, of course.'

'People will ask where I've gone,' said Isabella.

'Perhaps,' replied Mr Rudulfus. 'Perhaps not. But if they do, I have no doubt it will be blamed on the Schwartzgarten Slayer.'

'What if the Slayer *doesn't* want to kill you?' suggested Isabella desperately. It was a struggle to speak; it felt as though her lips were fusing together.

'But I'm quite certain that he *does* want to kill me,' said Mr Rudulfus. 'I have seen him tamper with this very box. I was observing him from behind the portrait of Marshal Borgburg in the Gallery of Oddities. I watched his every move.'

Osbert's heart was now beating so loudly that he

was certain the noise would attract Mr Rudulfus's attention.

'There is a small lever inside the box,' said Mr Rudulfus. 'Perhaps you can feel it?' Isabella nodded slowly. 'One tug of that lever, and the false bottom of the Star Box should open, as if by magic.' Isabella pulled at the lever, but of course, nothing happened. 'The mechanism has been jammed with a small wedge,' explained Mr Rudulfus, his face flushing with anger. 'So I would have been unable to escape, trapped inside until the charge of gunpowder roasted me to death.'

Isabella attempted to reply, but could not. Her lips were stuck fast.

'That will be the glue working,' said Mr Rudulfus. Isabella stared pleadingly at the man. 'The Rudulfus Grin,' he added with a self-indulgent smile. 'Let me explain,' he continued. 'I was fortunate to discover a box on the banks of the River Schwartz.' He opened a small case, and lifted out Osbert's reel of violin string and the instruction manual for the Industrial Strudel Machine. 'Clues,' he explained. 'Perhaps not incriminating clues, until you see this.' He brandished Osbert's pocketbook in his hand. 'It was damaged by river water, but I dried it carefully. You might be interested in the name inscribed inside the cover.' He took delicious pleasure in reading out the words, '*Osbert Brinkhoff.*'

Osbert gasped. His grip weakened on the rungs of the ladder and he slipped backwards, only steadying himself just in time to avoid tumbling down into the passageway below.

'And when the police find these clues, here beneath the stage, they too will discover the true identity of the Schwartzgarten Slayer,' continued Mr Rudulfus, still oblivious to Osbert's presence. 'You might be wondering why I did not claim the Governor's reward of five hundred imperial crowns? The answer is simple. I have withdrawn a hundred times the amount from the Bank of Muller, Baum and Spink. And tonight I will flee the city.' The merest hint of a smirk flashed across his face. 'I think it is important you understand my actions, to fully appreciate your fate.'

He put on his wig and hat and once more wrapped the fox-fur stole around his neck, preparing for a sudden departure.

Quickly and quietly, Osbert climbed up the ladder into the chamber. Slinking through the shadows, unseen by Mr Rudulfus, he crouched behind the Star Box, reaching out a hand to seize the bottle of chloroform that the teacher had foolishly left on the ground.

'Now, Isabella,' whispered Mr Rudulfus. 'As soon as I hear my cue from the stage above, I shall press this button.' He pointed to a red button on the side of the Star Box. 'The button activates the motors of the trap door and you will be lifted up onto the stage. The rest, I am sure, you have worked out for yourself. After all, you are an intelligent girl.' He smiled strangely. 'Now we wait.'

Three loud knocks from above were the cue Mr Rudulfus was waiting for.

'It is time for the Princess of the Festival to make an explosive entrance,' he giggled, slipping the raven mask over Isabella's head.

He reached out to press the red button. As he did so, Osbert leant forward from the shadows to remove the wedge that had jammed the mechanism at the bottom of the Star Box.

'Now pull the lever,' whispered Osbert, as Mr Rudulfus was distracted by a burst of impatient applause from above.

Isabella did as she was told. She pulled the lever and the secret door at the bottom of the box swung open, dropping her onto the cobbled ground below.

'This will not do,' muttered Mr Rudulfus, picking up the fallen wedge and jamming the secret door shut. He hauled Isabella up the steps of the ladder and deposited her back inside the Star Box.

Another three stamps from above, more impatient than before. Again Mr Rudulfus reached out for the red button, but once more the bottom of the Star Box swung open, bumping and bruising Isabella as she fell to the ground.

'The panel should be jammed,' hissed Mr Rudulfus. 'You ought to be trapped inside, unable to escape.'

Angrily, he jammed the secret panel of the Star Box as before and climbed up to see what was causing the problem. But as he leant in, he was pushed hard from behind and fell sprawling into the box. As he struggled up onto his knees, a pad of chloroform was held over his mouth, and he slumped forward.

When Mr Rudulfus awoke moments later, he discovered that he had been secured inside the Star Box, his head poking through the hole at one end of the box, his feet protruding through the two holes at the other end and his hands flapping helplessly at either side. He pulled at the hidden lever, but the secret door was safely secured by the wedge. He attempted to cry for help, but found that he could not. His lips were gummed together. Osbert held up the tin of Grin Gum in explanation. Isabella watched silently from the shadows, bruised and trembling.

Meanwhile, the crowd in the carnival tent above were growing impatient, and the Master of Ceremonies was stamping desperately on the stage.

Osbert reached inside Mr Rudulfus's case to recover the incriminating evidence – the violin string, the pocketbook and the instructions for the strudel machine. He also took out a stick of red greasepaint and a grey beard and moustache of crepe hair.

'So *you* were the museum custodian,' said Osbert,

staring at the make-up in disbelief. 'That's why you didn't want me to come too close. In case I recognised you beneath the disguise.' Mr Rudulfus could not speak a word but his eyes glinted with malevolence. 'You wanted me to tamper with the Star Box. You tried to catch me,' said Osbert, slipping the raven mask over Mr Rudulfus's head. 'You thought you were cleverer than me. I hope you know now that you are not.'

He pressed the red button, a bell rang and the platform began to rise. Taking Isabella by the hand, Osbert led her down the iron rungs into the tunnel below, pulling the cover to the passageway closed behind them.

Mr Rudulfus struggled as he stared up at the opening trap door. Slowly, the Star Box emerged onto the stage above.

—◆—

Osbert and Isabella were able to return to the carnival tent unseen; the audience were too engrossed in the activity on stage to notice them. Isabella took her place on the Festival throne, and Osbert sat back down next to Nanny.

The Star Box was in position, the fuse had been ignited, but the frantic wriggling of Mr Rudulfus, still wearing the raven mask, suggested to the audience that his plans to disappear into thin air had been thwarted.

'He's forgotten how to do it!' crowed Nanny.

The fuse spat and fizzed, slowly making its way towards the Star Box and the charge of gunpowder contained within. But Mr Rudulfus could not cry for help; his lips were still tightly glued together by the Grin Gum. The more he wriggled, the more unstable the box became. He kicked his feet desperately, but this served no purpose other than to dislodge the wooden wedges that secured the wheels of the box.

The Star Box began to roll towards the front of the stage, gathering speed. There was pandemonium in the tent; the guildsmen fled their booths, upsetting the tables in their haste, so the floor was awash with spiced rye beer. The Principal staggered to his feet and hurried from the tent, beating a path through the crowds with violent swipes of his cane.

'Get out of my way!' he screamed. 'Move, curse you!'

The Porter, who had been waiting patiently outside, cranked up the engine of the motorcar. The Principal climbed inside, fearing for his own life, and was driven swiftly away from Edvardplatz and back to the safety of The Institute.

All the while the Star Box glowed with the bright intensity of a comet. The Grin Gum fastening Mr Rudulfus's lips had begun to melt in the heat, and the accordion player rushed to the front of the tent, playing his music as loudly as possible to drown out the awful sound of the teacher's muffled screams. Desperate to douse the fuse before the gunpowder exploded, the assistant picked up a glass and splashed the contents on the Star Box. The fuse flared violently.

'You fool,' screamed the Master of Ceremonies, snatching the glass from the assistant. 'That's apple schnapps, not water!'

Nanny gripped Osbert's hand tightly and screwed

her eyes shut. But Osbert showed no such signs of squeamishness; Nanny almost had to drag him from the tent. Mrs Brinkhoff hurried behind, wheeling Mr Brinkhoff's invalid chair over the cobbles.

As they passed outside into the clear night air, Osbert was glad to see that Isabella's throne had already been carried out by her retinue of soldiers. She had also been reluctant to leave, watching as the Star Box flared up with bright orange flame.

Isabella's face was white and her heart beat rapidly. It was only luck that had spared her from the Star Box. She had almost died, and it was all Osbert Brinkhoff's fault.

Bursts of gunpowder shot from the box, igniting the crates of fireworks that had been stashed behind the curtains, in preparation for the Grand Display of Illuminations in Edvardplatz. The last remaining audience members fled from the tent as the rockets and bangers erupted, shooting from their boxes in a glittering spray of gunpowder, and bursting like thunder cracks against the canvas roof of the carnival tent. The ancient material singed and crackled, creating a sparking patchwork of holes that revealed the glittering night sky above. As the flaps of canvas fizzled away to ash, the wooden columns that had once supported the roof toppled to the ground, tearing to shreds the last remaining scraps of the tent. The crackle and burst of the fireworks gave way to an eminently more sinister noise, as a murder of ravens took to the skies, circling Mr Rudulfus as he kicked and struggled in the Star Box. He had finally shaken the raven mask from his head and the heat had at last melted the gum that secured his lips.

'It was Osbert Brinkhoff,' he squealed. 'Osbert Brinkhoff did this to me! Osbert Brinkhoff is the Schwartzgarten Slayer!'

But his voice could not be heard above the roar and crack of the fireworks. The ravens swooped down from above. 'Damn you!' he cried. 'Curse you!' The birds pecked at his head, his hands and his feet, seemingly impervious to the heat of the flames, which were fanned by the icy night breeze.

'I told him there'd be ravens,' confided Madame Irina to the Master of Ceremonies as they cowered behind the boiled beef and pickle stall.

There was nothing that could be done to save Mr Rudulfus. Wriggling to the last, he burned to death, still trapped inside the cracking, splintering hulk of the Star Box, pecked by the ravens till the life had drained from him.

———

The next morning, to mark the occasion of Mr Rudulfus's demise, Osbert left a parcel on Isabella's doorstep containing the tin of Grin Gum, and then headed for home.

'Another death,' shouted the blind newspaper seller. 'Another teacher slain.'

Meanwhile, in the Old Town, the Principal was arriving outside Mr Rudulfus's house, in the company of Mr Spink, the Inspector of Police and two bank cashiers.

'I thought I was acting for the best,' murmured Mr Spink, who had alerted the Principal's attention to Mr Rudulfus's withdrawal from the bank. 'It seemed a large amount of money to take out, but he assured me that he was acting in accordance with your wishes.'

'Silence,' demanded the Principal as the Inspector unlocked the door with a skeleton key.

They entered the darkened hall. There was an unpleasant aroma of rotting food, and this was explained by the roosting ravens on every stair, chair and bookcase. It was not even a day since the death of Mr Rudulfus, but the birds had already colonised his house. The floor was thick with raven droppings, and the party stepped carefully from room to room.

'In here,' said the Inspector at last, opening the door to Mr Rudulfus's study.

The ravens uttered a deathly murmur as the Principal entered. The cash boxes had been stacked neatly in the corner.

'What is this?' said the Principal, peering hard at strange markings that had been drawn upon the walls of the room.

'Looks like a map,' said the Inspector.

Mr Rudulfus had made an intricate drawing of the web of passages and sewers that ran beneath the streets of Schwartzgarten, which enabled him to avoid exposure to ravens wherever possible. *No ravens here*, he had scrawled in tiny, spidery writing, marking the safest points to re-emerge from the underground passageways.

'You know what to do, Spink,' said the Principal.

Mr Spink clicked his fingers and the waiting cashiers retrieved the cash boxes to be returned to the vaults of the bank.

A large raven perched on the mantelpiece gave a low and guttural caw and stretched its wings.

'Fear makes men do peculiar things,' said the Principal, turning towards the door. 'We will not speak of this again.'

⎯⎯◆⎯⎯

The Star Box itself survived but was so badly damaged that Schroeder the undertaker thought it best to bury it, body and all. As the pallbearers carried the charred remains of the box towards the gaping entrance to the mausoleum, a rattling could be heard from inside the box. The pallbearers stopped and all was silent.

'There's something trapped inside,' wheezed the undertaker.

'Shake it again,' suggested the Coroner.

The pallbearers shook the Star Box, and the noise could be heard as before.

'Harder!' roared the Principal.

The pallbearers rocked the box from side to side, so hard that Schroeder feared the blackened wood might split open, spilling the scorched remains of Mr Rudulfus onto the icy ground. Irritated, the Principal crouched beneath the box, staring up through a splintered hole in the wood.

'Again!' shouted the Principal. The pallbearers shook the box once more, and as they did so, a small, blackened lump dropped out through the hole, landing neatly in the Principal's outstretched hand.

'What is this?' he whispered to the Coroner.

'It's his heart,' said the Coroner, smiling awkwardly.

The Principal staggered to his feet, holding the heart away from him, seized by an unimaginable sense of terror. And as he did so, a raven swooped from the blackening sky and grasped the charred heart of Mr Rudulfus in its outstretched claws.

'Come back, you foul beast!' screamed the Principal, as the bird took to the skies. But the raven seemed reluctant to return, and swooped three times above the assembled funeral party, before settling at the top of a poplar tree, where it pecked contentedly at the burnt heart of Mr Rudulfus.

And so the heartless body of Mr Rudulfus was interred inside the mausoleum and the door sealed. The mourners departed, leaving behind the undertaker's son, who waited patiently beneath the poplar tree. It was not until nightfall that the raven tired of its ghoulish meal and, with a final violent shake, flung the heart down into the cemetery below, where it was speared on one of the wrought-iron spikes surrounding the tomb of Marshal Berghopf. With a dustpan and brush, the undertaker's son scooped up the charred remains, which he wrapped in his pocket handkerchief before returning home.

The next day, the funeral party returned to the cemetery. In his hands, Schroeder clutched a small ebony box; a brass plaque had been engraved with the words *The Heart of Aristotle Rudulfus*.

As it was hardly practical to unseal the mausoleum for such a small burnt offering, the box was dropped in a shallow hole beside the tomb and covered with soil.

From that day forth, ravens were often to be found on the grass there, pecking at the earth as if to torment the man in death as they had done in life.

Although spectacular, the manner of Mr Rudulfus's death was less than satisfactory to Osbert. It was through luck, rather than judgement, that the tutor had been despatched. And worse still, it had imperilled the beautiful Isabella.

However, Osbert was amused to discover a happy and coincidental postscript to the death of Mr Rudulfus, even though he could not justly claim responsibility. The mathematics teacher, Anatole Strauss, was so distressed by the explosive departure of Mr Rudulfus that he was driven quite insane, convinced that his own untimely end was imminent. He was often to be found wandering the cobbles of the city, his once waxed moustache drooping miserably, his Homburg hat battered and torn.

'His mind is quite gone,' said Doctor Zimmermann gravely.

'He just weeps and wails,' said Anatole Strauss's housekeeper. 'And I don't like it.'

Doctor Zimmermann nodded. 'I am quite certain that in due course the man's heart will break.'

One icy morning, just a week after the funeral of Mr Rudulfus, as Strauss crossed the street close to Edvardplatz, his foot caught in one of the rusted rails that ran between the tramlines and had once carried Prince Eugene's mechanical horse. As he attempted to extricate himself, he could hear the unmistakable sound of a tram rounding the corner and the conductor sounding the bell. Strauss's face was pale grey with terror as the driver frantically applied the brakes. But it was too late.

In the end it was not Anatole Strauss's heart that broke; it was his neck.

Chapter Fourteen

THE INSTITUTE lay silent. The Principal walked the empty corridors, peering through the windows into the now-empty classrooms of his deceased colleagues. He was a cadaverous man, a walking skeleton, who looked so ravaged by time, so poisoned by contempt for those around him that it seemed every painful breath he took might well be his last.

The deaths of Mr Rudulfus and Anatole Strauss in such quick succession had shaken him to the core, and as the weeks passed, the Principal had retreated further and further into the dark recesses of The Institute. His face had a haunted look and his eyes were sunken, as though pressed into the withered husk of his head.

Matters had gone from bad to worse. Even the Porter had been conscripted to teach lessons, which he did with a grim satisfaction.

But nevertheless, many parents had removed their children from The Institute, deciding instead to send them to boarding schools beyond Schwartzgarten, or teaching them at home, where they could keep a sharp eye on their offspring. Mr and Mrs Myop, however, who were always rather alarmed by the intelligence of their precocious daughter, continued to send Isabella to The Institute.

With steely determination, realising that without new teachers The Institute would be forced to close its doors, the Principal placed an advertisement in the newspapers and journals, appealing for teaching staff.

Pleasant and progressive academic institution seeks strong–willed and resilient replacement teaching staff. Favourable rates of pay. Applications in writing.

But stories of the dark events in Schwartzgarten had spread far beyond the city. Nobody was taken in by the Principal's lies. There was only one applicant, someone who had not signed his name, but had simply written his initials: A. M. L.

As the Principal entered his office to interview the

applicant, the man was standing at the window, staring out across the courtyard, his back turned towards the door. There was something in the air that unsettled the Principal: the unmistakable aroma of almond oil.

The man turned from the window and in the dimly lit room the Principal could just make out the face of Augustus Maximus Lomm.

———◆———

That evening, as Mrs Brinkhoff and Nanny prepared dinner, there was a gentle knock at the apartment door. Mrs Brinkhoff opened the door and peered into the gloom. The electric bulb on the landing flickered and crackled, casting just enough light to distinguish the shape of Mr Lomm, dressed in a black felt overcoat with a muffler round his neck. He bowed his head politely.

'Mrs Brinkhoff, I don't know if you'll remember me. We met once on Edvardplatz—'

'Remember you?' replied Mrs Brinkhoff, her eyes sparkling in the electric light. 'Of course we remember you, Mr Lomm. Please, please come in.'

Mr Lomm shook the rain from his umbrella and stepped into the apartment. 'And how is Mr Brinkhoff?' he inquired.

Mrs Brinkhoff shook her head, sadly. 'Bad,' she replied.

'But there's always hope,' said Mr Lomm, tenderly.

Mrs Brinkhoff nodded and knocked gently at Osbert's door. 'Osbert,' she whispered. 'There's somebody out here who would like to see you very much.'

For a moment Osbert hesitated. Was it the Inspector of Police waiting outside the door for him? Had he been careless and left another clue? Slowly, Osbert turned the handle and opened the door.

Stepping out into the sitting room, he could not believe his eyes. There, standing in front of him on the threadbare rug, was Mr Lomm.

'Is it really you?' whispered Osbert, half-afraid that if he raised his voice the image would vanish into thin air.

Mr Lomm laughed. 'Yes, it's me.' He removed his spectacles and wiped the greasy smears of rain from the lenses. 'And how have you been?'

Osbert was not quite sure how to answer. He wanted to tell Mr Lomm that he was very much better, that killing three of his teachers had made him happier than he had ever been. But he was certain that this was not a sensible thing to do. After all, what would Mr Lomm say? Would he agree that each and every one of the tutors deserved their untimely fate, or would he pick up the telephone and call for the police?

'I'm very well, thank you,' said Osbert.

'And how you've grown,' said Mr Lomm. This was not entirely true. Osbert had grown far less than other children of his age, but nevertheless Mr Lomm's words worked their magic, and Osbert glowed proudly.

Mr Lomm's face grew serious, and he stared earnestly at Osbert. 'I understand from the Principal that you are no longer a student at The Institute.'

Osbert shook his head.

'This was wrong,' continued Mr Lomm. 'Your exam score was quite remarkable. There was no earthly reason you should have been denied the Constantin Violin. I argued your case, but I'm afraid…' He stopped. 'You know the rest, of course.'

He laughed, self-consciously, and turned to Mrs Brinkhoff. 'I have resumed my position at The Institute, and I hope that in time things will improve. It is my greatest wish that Osbert should return to the school. But in the meantime, I shall be taking private violin students.' He smiled at Osbert. 'I hope very much that you might consider me as your new violin tutor?'

'I'm afraid we don't have any money for lessons,' said Mrs Brinkhoff, apologetically. 'But perhaps if I could work extra shifts at the glue factory—'

'No, you don't understand,' interrupted Mr Lomm, deeply embarrassed. 'I don't want any money. I think tutoring Osbert is very least I can do. I'm living above Salvator Fattori's delicatessen on the Avenue of Thieves. If Osbert is willing, I shall begin lessons tomorrow at six in the evening.'

—•—

At five-thirty the following day, after finishing work

for Oskar Sallowman, Osbert set off for his first violin lesson with Mr Lomm. The delicatessen's shop was located close to the Zoological Gardens, in a district known as Traitor's Gate. The Principal was so desperate for teachers that Mr Lomm was able to demand a higher rate of pay, and was no longer forced to live in the dank, mouldy basement of The Institute.

Osbert opened the door to the delicatessen, and the bell jangled noisily. It was a dark shop, made all the darker by the large smoked hams and salamis that hung from hooks in the ceiling.

'Yes?' said Salvator Fattori, heaving into sight behind the long mahogany counter.

'I'm here to see Mr Lomm,' replied Osbert. 'I have a violin lesson.'

There was a clattering from the depths of the shop, and Mr Lomm appeared from behind a large leg of pork.

'Osbert!' he cried, beaming. 'Welcome.'

'Take a bit of this with you,' said Salvator Fattori, cutting three thick slices of garlic sausage, wrapping them in paper, and handing them to Osbert.

'Thank you,' said Osbert, who always seemed to get on well with butchers.

Mr Lomm led the way upstairs to a small room with bare wooden floorboards and very little furniture. The only colour in the room was provided by a large vase of yellow silk tulips on the windowsill.

'I'm not sure if you remember the day I first showed you this,' said Mr Lomm, opening a cupboard, and taking out the familiar battered blue instrument case. 'It was the first violin I was ever given.' He passed the violin to Osbert. 'Perhaps you might like to look after it for me?'

Standing in Mr Lomm's room, playing his teacher's precious violin, it felt to Osbert as though nothing bad had ever happened. But he knew he had to continue with his task. While the Principal lived, Osbert's work was not complete. As his mother often said, 'The job worth starting is worth finishing.'

Meanwhile, at the Department of Police, the investigation into the mysterious Schwartzgarten slayings had ground to a halt. Of course, the Inspector had considered the possibility that Mr Lomm was responsible for the grisly deaths that had plagued Schwartzgarten, or more specifically, The Institute. After all, the man clearly had a motive. But as Mr Lomm had been working in a school on the shores of Lake Taneva and had an alibi for each of the murders, the Inspector grudgingly struck the name from his list of suspects.

A new chapter began at The Institute. The dark clouds had lifted a little with Mr Lomm's return. No longer would the kindly tutor be forced to hide his compassionate teaching methods at the school, and could tell stories to his heart's content. The children were fed on chocolate instead of fish stew and the peppermint cordial flowed freely.

But still, every morning the Principal would count the children into school, squinting from his tiny window high above the courtyard. And every evening he would count the children back out again. He was taking no chances. At night, as the hall clock struck ten, the Principal and the Porter would meet in the courtyard. Together, by the light of an oil lamp, they would chain and padlock the school gates. The police constables who stood guard outside the gates during the day would then be dismissed, hurrying down the hill and back into the city to return home for supper.

Retreating into the darkest depths of the building, the Principal would finally lock his study door, carefully sliding the bolts into place.

One particularly cold night two weeks after the return of Mr Lomm, and according to his routine, the Principal returned to the safety of his study and fastened the door behind him. All day he had been seized by a morbid sense of his own impending mortality, and arranged for the Porter to add an extra lock to the door. As he slid the final iron bolt into place, he let out a long gasp of relief. The wind howled through the room, rattling the windowpanes and ruckling the ancient tapestries which decorated the walls.

The Principal stood on the tiger-skin rug beside the blazing fire, watching as the fir branches cracked and hissed in the flames. He clacked irritably to himself, impatiently awaiting the telltale rattle of the lift pulley, which would signal the arrival of his dinner as it lurched upwards in the dumb waiter from the kitchen far below his private rooms.

Meanwhile, the Porter was polishing the Principal's limousine with beeswax and coconut oil when the bell rang from the entrance gate.

'As if I haven't got anything better to do with my time,' the Porter muttered to himself, as he set off across the courtyard. A small figure awaited his arrival, standing silently outside the gates.

'Who are you and what do you want?' demanded the Porter.

The figure took a step forward. It was a small man in a long overcoat and leather gloves, with a grey beard and moustache. He wore a hat and spectacles, and when he smiled he revealed a set of grey teeth. He held in his hands a bottle of schnapps, which he passed through the gates into the grateful, grasping hands of the Porter. There was a label tied with a bow.

'What's all this?' said the Porter, peering at the label in the murky half-light, and slowly making out the message: *A sample from the Brammerhaus Schnapps Distillery. Please enjoy with our good wishes.*

The Porter's mouth curled upwards to form a crooked and unpleasant smile. 'It's a cold night,' he said. 'Why shouldn't I have a little drop?' He pulled out the cork with his teeth and took a sniff. 'Apple schnapps. Good. Very good.'

He sipped from the bottle, and smiled. He took another sip. By the third sip he was out cold on the ground.

Osbert slipped out of the overcoat, took off his moustache and beard and removed the grey false teeth. He reached through the gates and unhooked a key from the Porter's waist. Osbert unlocked the gates and entered the courtyard. He emptied the bottle of schnapps, and placed it in his hunting cape. Slinking through the shadows, he slowly made his way towards the foreboding grey edifice of The Institute.

In the kitchen, the housekeeper bustled from larder to stove as butter hissed in a small copper pan. She opened the hatch of the dumb waiter and loaded on a beautiful silver duck press and a steaming dish of buttered beetroot. She slammed the hatch shut and pulled on the rope, sending the lift up to the Principal's rooms. Every movement was closely observed by Osbert as he peered in through the kitchen window. It was clear the Principal wouldn't be going to his grave on an empty stomach.

Upstairs, the Principal hovered expectantly by the hatch of the dumb waiter. The pulley creaked from below and his nostrils twitched at the delicious aroma of broiled duck as the steam curled and snaked its way up the lift shaft towards him. He took the tray and sat down at the dining table, cutting thick tender slices of the duck and heaping them onto his plate. He dropped the duck carcass into the press, turning the screw and listening with satisfaction as the bones cracked inside the gleaming silver contraption. Twisting the tap at the base of the duck press, he watched with delight as the juice from the bones dribbled out onto his plate.

Outside, as the effects of the drugged schnapps began to wear off, the Porter finally woke to discover that the key to the gates was no longer in his possession.

'It's gone,' he moaned, frantically searching the courtyard by the light of his oil lamp.

As the housekeeper prepared the Principal's dessert of cinnamon dumplings, there came a desperate knock at the kitchen door.

'Who is it?' called the housekeeper, half-afraid that the Schwartzgarten Slayer lurked outside.

'It's me,' answered a wheezy voice. 'Porter.'

The housekeeper unlocked the door, her heart beating hard in her chest. 'What's wrong?'

'It's lost,' he wailed. 'Gone.'

'Gone? What's gone?' asked the housekeeper. 'Have you been drinking?'

'That's got nothing to do with it,' snarled the Porter. 'The key to the gates. I had it, and now I haven't. It's vanished. When the Principal gets to hear of this…' Again he wailed.

'Well, what do you want me to do about it?' demanded the housekeeper.

'Come and help me look for it,' snapped the Porter.

The housekeeper ran outside to help, and in her hurry she forgot to lock the door behind her.

The Porter and the housekeeper scrambled round on their hands and knees, trying in vain to find the key that was now safely tucked away in the pocket of Osbert's hunting cape. The boy, who had been waiting patiently in the shadows outside, crept in through the kitchen door, bolting it securely behind him. He climbed into the lift, closed the hatch, and began tugging at the rope.

The Principal was enjoying a second helping of the pressed duck when he heard the familiar squeak of the pulley inside the wall as the dumb waiter approached his rooms from the kitchen far below. Angrily, he jumped to his feet, and screamed into the speaking tube. 'It's too soon for dessert. The duck's not finished while there's juice in its bones!'

But still the dumb waiter rattled up the lift shaft.

'Too soon!' screeched the Principal. 'Too soon!'

The lift came to a clattering halt. Enraged, the Principal wrenched open the door, and there, staring back at him, was Osbert Brinkhoff.

'But...but...how?' stammered the Principal. 'The Institute was locked and secured. No one could have gained entry. *No one.*'

Osbert smiled. 'Not even the Schwartzgarten Slayer?' he inquired politely.

The Principal staggered back in horror, stumbling noisily against the table. As Osbert climbed out of the lift, the man backed further into the room. There was no escape.

With a superhuman effort, the Principal seemed to gather his wits, assuming the air of a genial host.

'Please,' he said, smiling obsequiously and motioning towards a leather wingback chair. The Principal had been taken off guard. Only by stalling his night-time visitor could he hope to formulate a counterstroke. 'Do sit down,' he continued. 'I think we should talk.'

Osbert did as he was told and sat very still, observing his prey narrowly. The plan for despatching his victim was vague, but he was sure that the cleaver would show him the way; it seemed to burn in the pocket of his hunting cape, pleading to be used.

The skin on the Principal's face was paper-thin, pulled so tight over his skull it made his eyes look as though they were bulging from their sockets.

'So, you are responsible for the Schwartzgarten slayings,' concluded the Principal, as he scrutinised the diminutive assassin sitting opposite him.

Slowly, Osbert nodded.

'You murdered *all* of them?' asked the Principal.

'Doctor Zilbergeld and Mr Rudulfus,' answered Osbert. 'Professor Ingelbrod's death was an accident. And it was just a happy coincidence that Anatole Strauss had his neck broken by a Reaper.'

'Will you kill me too?' inquired the Principal.

'Yes,' replied Osbert, grimly. '*Mortui non mordent.*'

'Dead men don't bite,' translated the Principal. 'Or to put it another way, dead men tell no tales. Your Latin is very good.'

'Thank you,' said Osbert.

'So you're my nemesis?' asked the Principal. 'You're here to destroy me?'

'Yes,' said Osbert, earnestly.

The Principal smiled. It was an unpleasant smile. His thin blue lips parted to reveal his blackened teeth. 'And how exactly are you going to kill me?'

'I shall cut you into little bloodied pieces with my gleaming cleaver,' said Osbert, honestly. At last a plan had formulated, brutal but beautiful in its simplicity.

Placing his hands on the armrests of his chair,

the Principal slowly rose to his feet, his eyes darting craftily towards Good Prince Eugene's rapier, which hung from a golden hook on the wall. He made a tentative step forward, leaning on his Malacca cane for support. But Osbert was too quick for him, and before the Principal could unhook the rapier, the boy had blocked his path.

Osbert reached into the large pocket of his hunting cape and seized the wooden handle of the cleaver. 'The time has come,' he said, pulling the cleaver from his cape. It glinted in the flickering firelight.

'It seems you don't understand,' said the Principal. He smiled, his thin lips splitting as he did so. He leant heavily on his walking stick. 'You have one more lesson to learn.' With a sudden flash of speed, he clicked the silver handle of his cane two twists to the left, one twist to the right, and withdrew a razor-sharp blade, which had been concealed inside the Malacca casing. *'Ars moriendi,'* hissed the Principal. 'The art of dying.'

Osbert stepped back and saluted, holding the blade of the cleaver to his face, as the Principal had taught him. But the Principal did not have honour on his mind, he merely wished to despatch his diminutive foe as swiftly as possible.

Osbert did not even have time to call '*en guarde*' before the Principal lunged, aiming the exquisite point of his sword straight at Osbert's heart. But the Principal had trained Osbert well and the boy deflected the blow; the weapon glancing from the polished blade of the cleaver, sending sparks flying into the air.

'Glissard, excellent,' hissed the Principal. 'And now for the repartee.'

He reached behind him, unhooked Good Prince Eugene's golden rapier from the wall and threw his Malacca cane to the floor.

As the Principal jabbed with the rapier, Osbert retreated, stepping back onto the slate hearthstone. There was a smell of burning tweed, and Osbert looked down to see the hem of his hunting cape sparking and singeing. The Principal made an aggressive lunge with his blade and Osbert neatly sidestepped his opponent's rapier, running back into the centre of the room. The Principal toppled forward, perilously close to the fire, lodging the tip of his blade in the red-hot embers. He pulled the sword from the grate, turning quickly.

'So you think you can escape, eh?' he whispered, malevolently. As he stepped forward he did not hear the burning spruce log as it tumbled from the fire and rolled out onto the rug, where it began to smoke and smoulder.

He made another lunge, pushing Osbert back into the darkest corner of the room. Although the Principal was a brilliant swordsman, Osbert had youth and agility on his side. He also had ingenuity. As he backed away from the Principal, he became aware of the large tapestry hanging behind him, embroidered with the same motto that had been painted on the gymnasium clock: *SI HOC LEGERE SCIS NIMIUM ERUDITIONIS HABES*.

At last the meaning became clear.

'If you can read this then you are over-educated,' cried Osbert.

'Die!' screamed the Principal, slashing wildly at Osbert with the golden blade of the rapier.

The tapestry was secured by two lengths of cord,

both badly frayed. All the time deflecting the rapier blows which rained down from above, Osbert felt behind him with his free hand and seized hold of the tapestry. He pulled hard and, sure enough, one of the cords snapped. The ancient tapestry began to sag, sending out a thick cloud of dust as it rippled and billowed.

'My eyes!' screeched the Principal, momentarily blinded by the dust.

Osbert pulled hard at the other end of the tapestry, which broke free from the ceiling. The Principal stumbled forward and was enveloped by the falling fabric. He took a step backwards, screaming furiously and lost his footing, falling back towards the dining table. And as he fell, he struck his head on the silver duck press and lay motionless on the tiger-skin rug, his fencing rapier by his side, snapped at its monogrammed tip. Osbert picked up the broken fragment of the Principal's rapier and put it in his pocket. He stood still for a moment, observing the scene of devastation before him.

The smouldering log had set fire to the rug, which

seemed to breathe new life into the moth-eaten tiger skin. Roaring with flame, the tiger skin had in turn set fire to one of the tapestries, which fizzled and sparked alarmingly; the fire had taken hold of the room. The heavy velvet curtains burnt and flapped at the open window. A pile of papers flared and crackled on the Principal's desk, sucked into the air by the breeze, and scattered across the room like singed and terrifying winged creatures. The leather-bound books hissed and spat as fingers of flame climbed the great mahogany bookcase beside the door.

Osbert had only one way out and that was the way he had arrived. Leaving the prone figure of the Principal to be claimed by the ravaging flames, he made his escape. His task was complete and his heart leapt at the thought. Quickly, he climbed back into the lift and began to lower himself down to the kitchen below. Already the choking grey smoke was beginning to billow out into the lift shaft. Time was of the essence.

Suddenly, the lift came to a juddering halt. Osbert tugged at the rope, but he was unable to move it. From above came a strange noise: it was the squeak of the rope, slowly running over the pulley. He felt the lift being pulled upwards, back towards the Principal's rooms and the blazing fire, which was now raging through the upper floors of The Institute. Desperately Osbert began to hack at the rope with the blade of the cleaver.

There came a voice from the hatchway of the lift shaft. 'I know you're down there,' hissed the Principal, venomously.

Again, the lift lurched upwards. The heat was unbearable and Osbert found it impossible to believe that the man had not already roasted alive. Fear clutched at his stomach as the lift rattled to a halt. There stood the Principal, his head bleeding, his clothes singed. He gave a diabolical grin. 'I didn't dismiss you from class, Brinkhoff!'

He lunged forward, the snapped end of his golden rapier pricking Osbert's shoulder and drawing a flow of scarlet blood, which leached out onto his still pristine white shirt.

Osbert winced with pain and held his hand to the wound.

'Out, boy!' screamed the Principal, seizing Osbert by the collar of his hunting cape and pulling him from the lift and into the burning room. With a slice of the rapier blade, the Principal cut the remaining threads of rope and sent the lift careering down to the kitchen below, where it cracked and splintered into jagged shards of mahogany.

'There's no escape for either of us,' snarled the Principal, struggling to be heard above the roar of the flames. He took a step forward and Osbert slashed desperately at the air with his cleaver.

'Don't come any closer,' he cried.

'Not so brave now, boy?' crowed the Principal.

As he took another step, Osbert flung the cleaver, which spun blade over handle, glinting in the firelight. He had aimed for the Principal's head, but it was a misjudged throw, and the Principal knew it. Cackling with glee he reached out and caught the handle of the spinning cleaver deftly in his hand. But his delight was short lived. He had overbalanced reaching for the cleaver and staggered backwards towards the gaping lift shaft. The cleaver and rapier clattered to the floor as he flapped his arms, frantically battling to remain upright. Osbert grasped his opportunity, running full-tilt at the Principal, and pushing him into the lift shaft. The man's arms flailed wildly, his fingernails grasping and clawing at the brickwork. He somehow gained a hold with his left hand and then his right, his fingertips white as they clung to the wooden frame of the shaft. Osbert stared down at the Principal.

'What was your reason for all this?' panted the Principal. 'Because we expelled you?'

Osbert shook his head. 'Because of the way you treated Isabella and my mother and father.'

'Your father,' wheezed the Principal. 'He had brains but no fight in him.'

'Why did you refuse him a place at The Institute?' demanded Osbert.

The Principal grinned. 'He had the highest score of any student who ever sat the entrance examination. Even higher than you.' The awful truth struck Osbert harder than any rapier. 'He was too clever. Denying him a chance to study at The Institute was the best way to crush his dreams.' He groaned, and struggled to keep his grip. The strength was draining from him. His voice suddenly trembled with fear. 'You don't have to do this, Brinkhoff.'

'You're wrong,' said Osbert. 'I do.' And with that, one by one, he prised the Principal's fingers from the wooden frame of the lift shaft.

The Principal screamed as he fell, his knuckles scraping, his fingernails tearing as he plummeted to the bottom of the shaft, where he was impaled on a splintered fragment of the shattered lift. Osbert watched from above as the Principal gave a final jerk and lay silent, a stream of blood trickling from his lifeless lips. At last, the man was dead.

The fire was now so fierce that the floorboards had buckled and split and the panes of leaded glass shattered in the window frames. Osbert gasped to catch his breath, stumbling blindly through the suffocating cloud of smoke which swirled wildly about him, fanned by the draught from the glassless windows. He sank to his knees, crawling along the floor where the smoke was thinnest. He was desperate to escape, but he could not leave without first removing any possible trace of evidence. His cleaver. Where was his cleaver?

An icy gust of wind lifted the shroud of smoke just long enough to reveal the fallen blade, glittering like polished gold in the firelight. Osbert lifted the Principal's broken rapier and seized the cleaver from beneath, tucking it safely in his pocket. He felt his way back across the smouldering rug, and clambered to his feet. Sitting at the entrance to the lift shaft he swung his legs over the precipice. Inside the shaft he could see a row of iron rungs, which had been used by the master stonemasons when building The Institute so many years before. Osbert had but one chance. Placing his hands by his side, he pushed himself from the wooden ledge and leapt towards the first iron rung. His hands seized the metal bar, but he could not get his grip; he slipped and fell. But as he fell, his hunting cape billowed around him, catching on a rusted metal rivet halfway down the shaft and abruptly halting Osbert's descent. Swinging from his parachute of Brammerhaus tweed, he felt around him in the darkness and discovered another rung. Holding on tightly, he reached below with his foot and found a toehold; he was safe.

Osbert unhooked his cape from the rivet and slowly made his way down the lift shaft.

———•———

It was Mrs Mylinsky who first noticed the orange glow on the horizon, high above the city. Flames had begun to leap from the windows of The Institute, turning the grey sky of Schwartzgarten ever greyer with the billowing smoke. The streets of the city were soon full of people making their way up the hill as the mighty edifice burned.

The heat of the fire was so intense that the Porter, still unable to find his key, had driven the Principal's motorcar full-tilt at the wrought-iron gates to escape. Now he secretly hoped that the Principal was dead, rather than face the consequences when the man discovered the mangled gates and the crumpled motorcar. The housekeeper was wailing hysterically, the Porter attempting to comfort her with plum brandy.

'I couldn't get back inside the kitchen,' she bawled at the Inspector of Police, who was struggling to regain his breath after running to the top of the hill. 'The door was locked and bolted. There was nothing that could be done. Nothing, I tell you.'

'I'm sure you did all you could,' said the Inspector, reassuringly.

'Perhaps it's just a terrible accident?' suggested the Constable.

The housekeeper stared at the man as if he were stupid and Massimo barked. 'A terrible accident? It's the Schwartzgarten Slayer, that's who it is. He'll be up there now, doing for the Principal. Before you can blink an eye he'll be butchered in his chair with his throat cut, and the liver and kidneys filleted out of him, you mark my words.'

The Inspector removed his overcoat and rolled up his sleeves, certain that the moment was ripe for heroic action.

'The fire's too strong,' said the Porter. 'You'll burn to ashes if you go in there now.'

'A well-argued point,' said the Inspector, stepping

back from the flames and re-buttoning his coat. Heroic action was one thing, but dying in the process was quite another. He was nothing if not a practical man.

'But the Principal's still inside!' shrieked the housekeeper.

There came a groan from the roof as the timbers buckled under the weight of the enormous stone gargoyles. The front wall of The Institute collapsed, crushing the statue of Julius Offenbach as the masonry crashed to earth. There was nothing that could be done but to watch as The Institute burned to the ground.

As the crowds departed, only Isabella remained. The destruction of The Institute was no accident, of that she was certain. But what had become of Osbert? She looked everywhere for him, treading as close as she dared towards the blazing remains of the building. Surely Osbert was dead? Isabella turned. There in front of her stood a small figure, its face and clothes stained with soot. She did not quite trust her eyes in the moonlight.

'Osbert?' she whispered.

The figure approached and held out its hand.

Isabella reached out and picked up the proffered object. It was the tip of a rapier blade, engraved with the monogrammed initials of Good Prince Eugene. It was the tip of the Principal's rapier. Isabella smiled.

'It's done,' said Osbert.

The next morning, as the Inspector of Police travelled by tram across the city to return to the smouldering remains of The Institute, he considered the events so far. Professor Ingelbrod had been starved to death, Doctor Zilbergeld had been chopped into tiny pieces by the strudel machinery, Mr Rudulfus had burnt to death in the Star Box, Anatole Strauss had been slain by a tram. And now the Principal was dead.

In desperation he bent down to examine the ground. After searching for some minutes, he discovered a set of small footprints, leading with short strides through the ashes. The pieces of the jigsaw finally seemed to slot together in his brain.

The Inspector of Police was without doubt that the person responsible for the murders was short in stature, hardly more than four feet in height. He beamed, confidently.

'We're looking for a murderous dwarf,' announced the Inspector.

— ·—

The only evidence that remained to remind passers-by that The Institute had ever in fact existed were the four stone gargoyles from the roof which had crashed to earth and now protruded through the ashes. Very little was found of the Principal, apart from a few blackened bones and the fractured blade of his rapier, tarnished but still glinting with gold.

As the hearse rolled by, carrying the Principal's charred bones to their final resting place, the citizens of Schwartzgarten lined the streets. The Institute's vice-like grip on the city had at last been broken.

The crowds swarmed into the cemetery as the Principal's coffin was carried into the mausoleum, adorned with a wreath of ivy. The Coroner, the undertaker and the Inspector of Police removed their hats, bowed respectfully and walked quickly from the cemetery as the sky suddenly turned black, like ink in water. The crowds departed.

Only Osbert and Isabella remained at the graveside, hidden from view by the monumental alabaster statue of the Grim Reaper. And there was joy in their hearts.

CHAPTER FIFTEEN

—◆◈◆—

A**ND SO** it was that Augustus Lomm began to teach the remaining children of The Institute in his front room, above Salvator Fattori's delicatessen. There was only a handful of children to begin with: Osbert, Isabella, Ludwig, Louis and Little Olena. But Mr Lomm felt certain that in time his new school would grow.

For a while at least, life appeared to return to normal. Osbert's task was complete and it seemed that he had covered his tracks well. It had been reported in the papers that a small set of fingerprints had been discovered on the blade of the Principal's rapier, but as Osbert's prints were not held on file at the Department of Police he was safe, as long as he remained beyond suspicion.

As the weeks passed and no further murders were committed, the Governor of Schwartzgarten decreed that the Slayer had fled the city. The Inspector of Police was not convinced, but the Governor demanded that the Inspector's bulging file on the Slayer was to be stamped *Case Closed*. The Governor did not believe in loose ends.

———

As Acting Principal of The Institute, Mr Lomm declared that Osbert and Isabella's examination scores for the Constantin Violin still stood. Although Osbert's score was higher than Isabella's, Lomm suggested that the worthy winner should be decided on the strength of their musical accomplishments alone.

The Institute was nothing but ash and fallen masonry, so it was decided that the concert should be held on the stage of the Schwartzgarten Opera House.

Every day, Osbert and Isabella would rehearse together, sometimes at the Myop home, and sometimes at Nanny's apartment. On the night of the recital, as Osbert practised his scales in the kitchen, Nanny bustled around the boy's bedroom, collecting dirty clothes to take to the laundry. A button dropped from Osbert's nightshirt and rolled under the bed, so Nanny crouched down on her hands and knees, mumbling irritably to herself. As her hand fumbled beneath the bed, she dislodged the loose plank where Osbert concealed his savings jars.

'*War Chest?*' read Nanny, curiously. Beside the jars was Osbert's hunting cape, neatly folded. Nanny tugged at the cape, and out fell Osbert's best white shirt, singed and stained with blood. And beneath the shirt was Osbert's cleaver, still covered in soot from the fire at The Institute. Nanny gasped.

'What are you doing?' said a voice.

Nanny turned and there stood Isabella, watching with interest.

'It's wicked to creep up on people,' said Nanny, quickly replacing the floorboard. 'You could have brought on a seizure.' She bundled the cape, shirt and cleaver into the laundry basket and hurried from the room.

—◆—

Osbert had never been inside the Opera House. It was an enormous hall, with a high raised stage. The ceiling was hung with cut-glass chandeliers and the walls were adorned with plaster figures of Schwartzgarten's greatest composers.

It was a cold night and Mrs Myop sat in the audience, wrapped up warmly in her mink coat. Embarrassed by the moth-eaten state of her own clothes, Mrs Brinkhoff turned up the sleeves of her coat so that Mrs Myop would not see the holes. Next to Mrs Brinkhoff sat Mr Brinkhoff, who had been wheeled to the Opera House in his invalid chair. Beside Mr Brinkhoff sat Nanny, turning over a hundred dark thoughts in her head as she contemplated Osbert's singed and bloodstained shirt.

As the Governor of Schwartzgarten took his seat in the royal box, silence fell over the assembled audience. The curtains were raised and Mr Lomm stepped out onto the stage, illuminated by a single spotlight. He coughed politely and gave a low bow to the Governor.

'Sir, citizens of Schwartzgarten. It is with immense pleasure that I welcome you to tonight's musical recital. The Schwartzgarten Imperial Orchestra will play Constantin Esterberg's first and, alas, last symphony. But first, it is my honour to present two of The

Institute's most exemplary students: Osbert Brinkhoff and Isabella Myop.'

Osbert and Isabella walked onto the stage, half-blinded by the bright lights. There was loud applause, which echoed round the vast concert hall like a clap of thunder. Mr Lomm opened the case of the Constantin Violin and carefully removed the priceless instrument.

'To begin this evening's competition recital, Osbert Brinkhoff, who will play "Death Comes A-Waltzing".'

Osbert lowered the stand and turned over the page of sheet music. Mr Lomm handed him the violin and he carefully oiled the bowstrings with a block of rosin.

Osbert placed the violin beneath his chin. The instrument smelt of wood polish and history. He could close his eyes and imagine at once that he had been transported back to the days when Constantin Esterburg himself entertained Prince Eugene.

As he played, Osbert felt the vibration of the strings, down through his left wrist and into his arm; it was as though the violin had become part of him. The mournful notes rose and fell, filling the Opera

House with an exquisite and intoxicating sense of gloom, enough to make a heart break, the music was so beautiful.

Isabella watched from the wings of the stage. She knew that Osbert would win, and the knowledge clawed at her stomach.

As Osbert lifted the bow from the strings there was silence. The entire audience had been hypnotised by the mournful beauty of his performance.

Mr Lomm broke the spell, clapping warmly and stepping forward to introduce Isabella. 'And next, Isabella Myop, who will play for you "In the Dark Woods of Schwartzgarten".'

'Good luck,' whispered Osbert, as Isabella walked to the front of the stage. Mr and Mrs Myop glowed proudly as their daughter took the Constantin Violin and began to play.

Isabella was an excellent violinist – her playing was faultless. But it lacked the depth of Osbert's performance. She had seen the way that Osbert's music could reach beyond the stage to bewitch the audience, but despite her best efforts, she could not cast that same intoxicating spell. And as she played a thought entered into her head, and no matter how hard she tried to shake it loose, the thought would not go away. The thought was this: that deep down she had grown to hate Osbert Brinkhoff.

'Very good. Excellent, excellent,' said Mr Lomm, smiling broadly as Isabella bowed before the audience. 'The Institute is very proud of you. Very proud of you both.'

Osbert and Isabella returned to their families. Mrs Brinkhoff squeezed Osbert's arm, and Mr Brinkhoff patted him on the head. Mr Lomm replaced the Constantin Violin in its case.

The musical director of the Opera House conferred with Mr Lomm. There was only one possible outcome.

The Governor of Schwartzgarten stepped onto the stage to make the presentation. Osbert and Isabella sat patiently in their seats.

'Good citizens of Schwartzgarten,' began the Governor. 'I need not tell you what an unusual time this has been. To see so many teachers slain in the most unimaginably gruesome ways. I feared that our children would become quite deranged from the awfulness of it all. But no. Here we are. And here I am. And here is Osbert Brinkhoff.'

Mr Lomm led Osbert from his seat and back up onto the stage. There was a lump in Isabella's throat and the blood seemed to boil in her veins.

'Take a bow, boy,' said the Governor. 'You have been awarded the Constantin Violin.'

Osbert smiled, hardly daring to believe what had happened. The Constantin Violin was his for a year. No longer would he have to content himself with gazing at the ancient instrument in its glass case; it was his to play whenever he wished.

Isabella stared at the floor, not looking her rival in the eye. As the audience applauded, Osbert whispered to his friend.

'Perhaps we could *share* the violin?'

But Isabella had no intention of sharing anything. As Osbert accepted the Constantin Violin from the Governor of Schwartzgarten, a plan was already formulating in Isabella's mind.

When Osbert returned home, he closed his bedroom door, reached beneath the bed and lifted the loose plank. He pulled out his savings jars.

'*War Chest*,' he smiled to himself, and removed the label. His tutors had been vanquished and he had no need for a war chest now. Instead the money could be spent on macaroons and lingonberry cordial, a consolation treat for poor Isabella. As he replaced the jar, he was suddenly gripped by a sense of dread. Where was his hunting cape and the bloodstained shirt? And where was his cleaver?

There was a gentle knock at the door and Osbert thrust the money jar beneath the bed sheets. Nanny entered the bedroom.

'Somebody has been in my room,' said Osbert, eyeing Nanny suspiciously.

'Maybe they have and maybe they haven't,' replied Nanny.

'Something's been taken,' continued Osbert.

'Maybe it has,' said Nanny. 'And if it has, maybe it's been hidden away where no soul will ever find it.' She patted Osbert on the arm.

He smiled back. 'Do unto others before they can do unto you,' whispered Osbert, and Nanny nodded in agreement.

—••—

Nanny would have protected Osbert to the end of time, but events were moving more quickly than even she could have predicted. The very next morning Isabella slipped silently from the Myops' pastry shop and climbed into a taxicab.

'The Department of Police, please,' said Isabella, clutching a box in her hands. She had gathered an interesting collection of mementos from the Schwartzgarten Slayer: the dried crumb of pastry from the Oppenheimer Strudel Factory, Mr Rudulfus's Grin Gum and the cracked tip of the Principal's fencing rapier. It was all the evidence she needed.

Arriving at the Department of Police, Isabella placed the box on the counter and lifted the lid.

'What's all this about then?' asked the desk sergeant, laughing nervously.

'Evidence,' said Isabella. 'Everything you need to

arrest the Schwartzgarten Slayer is contained inside this box.'

The desk sergeant telephoned upstairs to the Inspector of Police. The Inspector, whose wife had still refused to let him return home, was sitting at his desk, shaving in front of a pocket mirror. The telephone bell rang violently, and he nicked the side of his face with the sharp blade of his cutthroat razor.

'Damn it all!' he cried, answering the telephone with one hand and staunching the flow of blood with the other. 'Are you trying to give me a heart attack?'

'No, Inspector. Many apologies, Inspector,' spluttered the desk sergeant. 'It's just that a young girl has arrived with a box of evidence.'

'Evidence?' barked the Inspector. 'Evidence of what?'

The desk sergeant whispered into the receiver. 'The identity of the Schwartzgarten Slayer.'

The Inspector raced downstairs, buttoning up his jacket and straightening his hair. 'What's going on then?' he muttered, as he approached Isabella, who was waiting patiently. 'Wasting police time, I shouldn't wonder.'

The desk sergeant handed the Inspector the box. The Inspector stared inside, dumbfounded. He pulled out a small piece of twisted metal.

'I think it's from the Principal's sword,' said Isabella. 'I saw Osbert Brinkhoff drop this box in the street outside my parents' pastry shop. I expect it contains valuable clues. Perhaps,' she suggested, 'if you dusted for fingerprints?'

The Inspector gawped at the girl. 'You say you saw the boy drop this box?'

Isabella nodded. 'And perhaps,' she continued carefully, 'if you compare these fingerprints with the fingerprints you discovered on the rapier from The Institute, I think you'll find that they both belong to the same person.'

Many hours later, as darkness gripped the city, the Inspector of Police dragged himself up the stairs to the Brinkhoff apartment, wheezing and gasping as he reached each landing, wiping the perspiration from his head and neck with a large pocket handkerchief.

'It makes the blood run cold,' said the Inspector, as the Constable rang the electric bell to Nanny's apartment. It hardly seemed possible that a boy so young could be the perpetrator of the Schwartzgarten slayings. Yet Isabella Myop had been quite correct, the fingerprints on the Principal's sword which had been recovered from the smouldering remains of The Institute were a perfect match with those on the objects contained within Isabella's box of evidence.

Mrs Brinkhoff answered the door. 'May I help you?'

The Inspector of Police removed his hat and shifted awkwardly on the spot. 'It's about your son.'

'Yes?' said Mrs Brinkhoff. 'What about him?'

The Inspector hardly knew how to begin. 'We have reason to believe that young Osbert may be the Schwartzgarten Slayer.'

'You'd better come inside,' said Mrs Brinkhoff, wondering for a moment whether she was hallucinating from the fumes at the glue factory.

Mr Brinkhoff, who had overheard the Inspector, wheeled his invalid chair into the sitting room. 'Surely there must be a mistake?'

'Of course there must,' said Mrs Brinkhoff, shaking her head in bewilderment. 'It's incredible. Our darling Osbert, accused of four murders?'

'Show us the evidence!' demanded Nanny, disentangling her arms and legs from the moth-eaten blanket she slept under. She hauled herself up from the leather sofa and stood glowering at the Inspector, eyeball to eyeball. 'If you're going to come in here, waking an old woman with threats and accusations, show us all the proof!' She prodded the Inspector hard in the chest with a stumpy finger. 'That's what I say to you!'

'In due course,' said the Inspector, backing away, fearful that another of Nanny's prods would cause him serious injury. 'Now, may I see the boy?'

Quietly, Mrs Brinkhoff opened Osbert's bedroom door and gently shook her son awake.

'What is it, Mother?' asked Osbert, sitting up in bed. 'Is it Father? Is he ill again?'

'Put on your dressing gown, darling,' said Mrs Brinkhoff. Her mind was swimming. 'There are some people here that would like to talk to you.'

'Is it the police, Mother?' asked Osbert.

'Yes,' said Mrs Brinkhoff, disconcerted. 'But however did you know?'

'I just wondered,' said Osbert with a shrug.

As he tied the belt of his dressing gown he pondered the unfolding events. How had he been tripped up? Had he left another clue? Had Nanny betrayed him? And what could he do next? He stared up at the window. He contemplated jumping to the pavement below, but knew he would be smashed to pieces in the process. So instead he put on his slippers and walked out into the sitting room to face whatever Fate had in store for him.

The Inspector of Police could hardly believe that the small boy standing in front of him, dressed in slippers and dressing gown, was none other than the Schwartzgarten Slayer. And yet the evidence seemed to add up to one conclusion.

'Do you have anything to say?' asked the Inspector.

'Nothing,' replied Osbert grimly. He kissed his mother goodbye, and as he bent over to hug his father, he whispered to him. 'I know the truth, Father. You should have been given a place at The Institute. Your examination score was the highest the Principal had ever seen. Even higher than mine.'

Mr Brinkhoff gave a sad smile and clung so tightly to Osbert's arm that the Inspector had to prise them apart.

'Hold out your hands,' said the Inspector as the Constable opened a pair of handcuffs. But the handcuffs were so large that Osbert could easily slip his hands through the holes. Instead, the Inspector tied a chain around the boy's waist.

Nanny wrapped a scarf around Osbert's neck. 'I won't tell nothing that I know,' she whispered with a sly wink.

Mr and Mrs Brinkhoff watched sadly from the landing as the Constable led Osbert downstairs and out through the open front door.

It was an icy night, and the cobblestones in front of the apartment were treacherous underfoot. A small group of onlookers had gathered outside, chattering and cackling as the Inspector marched his prisoner to the police wagon, which stood waiting on the cobbles of Donmerplatz.

'I told you there was something not right about that family,' said the man in the dirty vest who had threatened to cut out Osbert's liver.

'Hacked to pieces in our beds,' agreed his wife. 'That's what would have become of us all!'

The driver cracked his whip and the wagon rolled slowly away.

—•—

By the time Osbert arrived at the Department of Police, news of his arrest had spread across the city and the street swarmed with people, eager to witness the arrival of the Schwartzgarten Slayer. Still leading Osbert by the chain, the Inspector of Police guided the boy inside.

The desk sergeant sharpened his pencil.

'Name?' he demanded.

'Osbert Brinkhoff,' replied Osbert.

'Age?'

'Twelve,' said Osbert.

'Twelve years old,' repeated the Inspector of Police, shaking his head in disbelief. 'Just a boy. And you really thought you could outsmart me, did you?'

'Yes,' replied Osbert. 'I thought there was every chance.'

The Inspector growled under his breath.

After entering Osbert's details in the ledger, the desk sergeant ushered the boy through a door and into a long, dark passageway lined with police cells. 'You'll be in cell number seventeen,' said the desk sergeant, pushing Osbert gently but firmly into a particularly grim little room.

'He's a slippery one,' said the Inspector to his men. 'A boy who can despatch four of his teachers in cold blood is a boy to keep a very close eye on.'

The door was locked, bolted and padlocked to make quite certain that Osbert could not escape.

———————

Mr Lomm, who could not afford to keep the fire blazing in the grate, had gone to bed early that night, but was woken at eleven o'clock by a loud banging at the shop door.

Salvator Fattori had long since shut up the delicatessen, and was snoring loudly in his bedroom.

By the light of a pocket torch, Mr Lomm made his way downstairs into the shop, arming himself with a clove-studded leg of pork, in case of intruders. Cautiously opening the shop door, he raised the leg of pork, ready to defend himself. But there were no intruders to be seen, only Isabella Myop, shivering on the freezing pavement.

'Whatever is it?' asked Mr Lomm, hiding the pork leg behind his back. 'What's happened?'

'It's Osbert,' said Isabella. 'He's been arrested.'

At first Mr Lomm laughed, until he realised that Isabella was in deadly earnest. 'Are you certain?' he asked.

Isabella held out the late edition of *The Informant*. Mr Lomm's lips moved silently as he read the headline: IS A TWELVE-YEAR-OLD BOY THE SCHWARTZGARTEN SLAYER?

Mr Lomm looked up, his spectacles misting over in the cold. 'You'd better come inside,' he said. 'Before you catch your death.'

Mr Lomm's hands shook as he turned the pages of the newspaper. His brain throbbed as he attempted to take in the full horror of Osbert's alleged crimes. The embers were dying in the grate, but it was enough for Isabella to warm herself. At last, Mr Lomm folded the paper and turned to the girl.

'But I can't believe it,' he insisted.

'But there it is, in black and white,' countered Isabella quickly. Mr Lomm pursed his lips, deep in thought. 'I suppose,' said Isabella, continuing carefully, 'if Osbert Brinkhoff is responsible for the deaths of so many people, the Constantin Violin should rightfully belong to me.'

Mr Lomm stared hard at Isabella, who smiled angelically back at him. 'I don't suppose there's any precedent for this.'

'I don't suppose there is,' replied Isabella.

Mr Lomm put on his hat and coat and prepared to walk Isabella home. 'And besides,' he continued, 'Osbert hasn't been found guilty. I'm sure this is all a perfectly innocent mistake.'

Isabella smiled pleasantly. But inside her head

her thoughts were not at all pleasant. It was vital, she concluded, that Osbert's guilt should be proved without any shadow of a doubt.

CHAPTER SIXTEEN

THE TRIAL of Osbert Brinkhoff was the most
unusual case the city of Schwartzgarten had
ever witnessed. The Governor, fearing that he would
be voted out of office at the next election if he didn't act
decisively, arranged for the notorious lawyer Septimus
Van der Schnell to prosecute at the trial. The only man
who had ever defeated Septimus in court was his own
brother, Octavius Van der Schnell.

Octavius was a kindly man with a soft heart and a
weakness for lost causes. But he was not cheap.

Apprehensively, Mr Lomm closed the delicatessen
door behind him and set off for the Bank of Muller,
Baum and Spink. Two days had passed since Osbert's
arrest and he could put off the evil day no longer. If he
was going to help Osbert, it was vital that he should
discover exactly how much money remained in The
Institute's meagre account. Mr Lomm was not certain
of Osbert's innocence, but he knew for a fact that the

Brinkhoffs were not able to pay for a lawyer of Octavius Van der Schnell's standing.

—◆—

'I shall call for Mr Spink,' said the cashier, pressing an electric bell beneath the counter.

Mr Lomm waited patiently in the banking hall, wiping the beads of nervous perspiration from his forehead.

The elevator appeared from the offices above, and Mr Spink emerged, a bright red carnation in his buttonhole.

'My name is Lomm,' spluttered the teacher anxiously. 'I am the Acting Principal of The Institute.'

'Of course, Mr Lomm,' said Mr Spink, nodding his head in approval. 'I've been expecting you. If you would kindly step this way?'

He led Mr Lomm to the elevator, and together they descended three floors to the bank's deepest vaults. They stepped out into a long, dark corridor with high ceilings. Mr Spink pressed a button and the corridor was dimly illuminated by electric light. The walls were lined with shelves, stretching from the floor all the way to the ceiling. Each shelf was piled high with neatly stacked deposit boxes of black-painted metal.

'Which box belongs to The Institute?' asked Mr Lomm, anxiously.

'All of them,' replied Mr Spink, greatly amused. He waved his hand towards the shelves. 'Pick a box.'

Mr Lomm closed his eyes and held out a hand, picking a box at random. He opened his eyes. His hand had alighted on box number OB00185. Mr Spink took the box from the shelf, and placed it on a small table.

'Well?' said Mr Spink, hardly able to suppress his excitement. 'Open it.'

He handed Mr Lomm a small golden key. 'This key opens all the boxes in the vault.'

Mr Lomm placed the key in the lock. It turned easily. He lifted the lid. The box was stuffed full of bank notes. 'Do all the boxes have so much money in them?' he croaked.

'No,' replied Mr Spink. 'Some have much more. And in some instances, jewellery, bank bonds, gold and silver ingots...'

Mr Lomm reached out a hand to steady himself against the table. 'But the Principal,' he gasped. 'He never put his hand in his pocket for anything. He wouldn't pay for a stove to warm my room in the winter. Not even when icicles started forming from the ceiling.'

'And that's why there's so much money in the vault,' said Mr Spink. 'He was a good investor, but a terrible, terrible man. I could hardly believe it when I discovered the Principal had burned to death. A very happy day.' His eyes sparkled merrily. 'The greater part of The Institute's money is made up from the Offenbach Bequest. After the late Julius Offenbach died so slowly and horribly in his bathtub, all his money was bequeathed to The Institute. And now, as the Acting Principal of The Institute, it is yours to do with as you wish.'

———◆———

Outside the courtroom the windows were frosted, but inside the ancient boiler system rattled and hissed behind the walls, heating the room until it was almost suffocatingly hot.

Osbert was led into the courtroom. He was not tall enough to look out over the top of the dock, so a clerk of the court brought him three leather-bound law books to stand on. As he climbed the tower of books and his head became visible, there was a gasp in the courtroom. Dressed in his very best clothes, with his blond hair neatly brushed into a side parting, Osbert looked very small and angelic, and not at all like a murderer standing trial for slaying four of his former teachers in cold blood and inadvertently sending a fifth to his doom beneath the wheels of a tram.

The visitors' gallery was so full that many people had to stand. Osbert's mother and father and Nanny sat sadly together, almost hidden from view, and at the very back of the gallery stood Isabella. Osbert smiled, but Isabella did not meet his gaze.

The clerk of the court stepped forward and banged his gavel on the desk. 'Court rise.'

A silence fell in the courtroom as the three judges entered the room and took their seats at the bench. Next came Octavius and Septimus, clutching their notes. They bowed to the judges and took their places.

The clerk called the first witness. 'Augustus Maximus Lomm.'

Mr Lomm stood in the witness box. It was so hot in the room that perspiration, mixed with almond oil, trickled down his face. He mopped his forehead with his pocket handkerchief as Septimus Van der Schnell approached the box.

'Do you believe that the boy is intelligent enough to have committed these crimes?'

Mr Lomm scraped back his hair, which had flopped over his spectacles as the almond oil melted in the heat.

'Of course he's intelligent enough,' replied Mr Lomm. 'But why would he? What possible reason would he have had for killing so many people in cold blood?'

And this was the unanswered question on everybody's mind.

'Next witness!' cried the first judge impatiently, wishing that it was still within his power to send children to the gallows.

That evening, Osbert stood alone in his prison cell, practising scales on the Constantin Violin. He heard a rattling of keys and lifted the violin bow from the strings.

'You've got visitors,' grunted the desk sergeant, unlocking the door to Osbert's cell.

Osbert put his violin back inside its case as Mrs Brinkhoff entered, smiling nervously. Behind her came Mr Lomm, and behind him bustled Nanny.

'I brought you this,' said Nanny, removing the lid from a steaming bowlful of apple dumplings.

'Thank you,' said Osbert, placing the bowl on the table.

Nanny handed him a shiny metal tablespoon. Osbert looked thoughtful, tidying his hair as he stared at his reflection in the back of the spoon.

His mother smiled sadly, as Osbert toyed with the apple dumplings. There was a long and uncomfortable silence, broken at last by Mrs Brinkhoff.

'Maybe if you tell them you're sorry—?' she began.

'But I'm *not* sorry, Mother,' Osbert interrupted. 'I'm glad they're all dead.'

'Could I speak to Osbert on my own?' asked Mr Lomm quietly.

Mrs Brinkhoff kissed Osbert gently on the forehead and stepped outside.

'You can take this, thank you' said Osbert, handing Nanny the bowl of apple dumplings. 'I don't feel very hungry.'

Nanny pushed the bowl back into Osbert's hands. 'Eat them all up like a good boy.' She winked at Osbert and followed Mrs Brinkhoff outside.

Mr Lomm sat on the broken chair in the corner of the cell. 'I see you're continuing to practise on the Constantin Violin,' he said approvingly.

Osbert nodded his head.

Mr Lomm paused, trying carefully to form his next sentence. 'A lot of very bad things have happened; there's no way to deny that. But whatever you did, I'm sure that you didn't do it entirely on your own.' He pursed his lips, waiting for an answer.

Osbert wanted to tell Mr Lomm everything. It hurt him to keep things from his beloved teacher.

It was clear that someone had discovered Isabella's collection of mementoes of the Schwartzgarten slayings, but Isabella could not be blamed for her carelessness. And besides, Osbert had made his pledge: he would always protect Isabella and he would take their secret with him to the grave.

'There's nothing more to tell you,' said Osbert, lowering his head unhappily.

'Time's up,' shouted the desk sergeant, rattling his keys.

Mr Lomm rose from his chair.

'Thank you,' said Osbert.

Mr Lomm smiled sadly. It was the last time he would ever speak to his protégé.

Osbert sat on his hard bed and lifted the lid from the bowl of apple dumplings. He dipped in with his spoon, and struck metal. Curiously, he reached beneath the dumplings and pulled out a small package wrapped in brown paper, which had been concealed at the bottom of the bowl.

He peeled back the wrapping and there inside was his beautiful, marvellous cleaver.

At ten o'clock the next morning the court reconvened.

'What we are looking for,' said Octavius Van der Schnell, 'is a *scoius criminis*. That is to say, a partner in crime. It seems quite incredible to believe that Osbert Brinkhoff carried out these bloody acts entirely on his own.'

As Octavius stared out across the courtroom, observing the effect of his speech, his gaze fell briefly on Isabella Myop, who gasped and bit her lip. He turned hopefully to Osbert. 'Well?'

Osbert glanced at Isabella. 'But I *did* do it on my own,' said Osbert. 'I killed every one of them.'

'What?' growled the first judge, malevolently.

'He admits it?' gasped the second judge.

The third judge scratched at the paper in front of him with the tip of his fountain pen, writing so vigorously that he upset his ink well, spilling the contents across the pages of his book.

'Of course I admit it,' said Osbert calmly. 'They deserved to die.'

The judges whispered to each other.

'Do you think he's mad?' asked the first judge.

'Mad or evil,' said the second judge.

'Diabolical to the core,' said the third judge.

They were in agreement.

The first judge turned to Osbert. 'We find the accused guilty of murder.'

'No!' yelled Mr Lomm from the visitors' gallery. 'He's just a boy!'

'Silence!' screamed the second judge.

'There must be some mistake,' continued Mr Lomm.

'We make no mistakes,' growled the third judge.

'Osbert Brinkhoff must have been temporarily unbalanced of mind,' argued Octavius, pleading for clemency.

'*Nemo repente fuit turpissimus*,' riposted Septimus, triumphantly. 'No one ever became extremely wicked suddenly.'

'His heart's as black as pitch!' screeched Mrs Myop, who had become quite deranged at the thought that Osbert had spent so much time with her darling Isabella.

Mrs Brinkhoff staggered to her feet and cried out. 'But what will happen to my darling little Osbert? What will *become* of him?'

Septimus smiled. 'The boy will be sent to the Schwartzgarten Reformatory for Maladjusted Children. He will have a padded cell all to himself.'

As Osbert was led away he nodded gratefully to Mr Lomm. He looked up to the gallery, where his father was comforting his mother. And there was Isabella, leaning over the balcony. She grinned at Osbert; the Constantin Violin was at last hers. Osbert did not understand. Was she happy that he had been found guilty? As he watched, the smile became a laugh, unseen by everyone but Osbert. Isabella Myop was *laughing* at him.

Three days later at seven o'clock in the morning, the desk sergeant carried a breakfast tray down the corridor to Osbert's cell. The man was not alone; he was accompanied by the Superintendent of the Schwartzgarten Reformatory for Maladjusted Children. She was a short and severe woman, with thick plaits of yellow hair coiled on either side of her head, which was as round and smooth as a cannonball. Every flat-footed step she took seemed to boom along the narrow passageway.

'One month in my care, and I'll wipe all thoughts of murder from the little poppet's head,' she boasted, cracking her knuckles in a way that set the desk sergeant's teeth on edge.

'This is the boy's cell,' he said, unlocking the door to the dark and dingy little chamber. 'Wake up, Brinkhoff. The Superintendent's here to cart you away.'

There was no answer. Osbert did not even stir in bed.

'I said, wake up!' barked the desk sergeant. He pulled back the woollen blanket, revealing nothing but a pillow and a bundled pile of clothes. Osbert Brinkhoff had gone.

The Inspector of Police was called. He ran panting down the corridor and into the cell. Pulling the bed to one side, the Inspector discovered a hole scraped away in the wall, just large enough for a small boy to squeeze through. Daylight was clearly visible through an air vent on the other side of the wall. There was a neatly piled heap of stone dust concealed behind the door of the cell. Beside it lay the discarded tablespoon that Nanny had given Osbert. Reaching his hand into the hole, the Inspector pulled out a final calling card:

With apologies for my sudden departure.
Sincerely,
The Schwartzgarten Slayer.

EPILOGUE

T HE MONTHS passed and the seasons changed. Mr Lomm, who was very prudent with money, arranged for a new school to be erected on the site of the old Institute. He did not touch the capital invested in the bank, and paid for the building work entirely from the interest that had accrued on the Offenbach Bequest.

Mrs Brinkhoff, who held herself personally responsible for Osbert's mental derangement, went to work at the Schwartzgarten Reformatory for Maladjusted Children. Mr Brinkhoff, though heartbroken, had recovered his health and returned to his position at the bank. He also began a correspondence course with the University of Brammerhaus, having finally discovered that he *was* a genius after all.

The Brinkhoffs, who had suffered greatly, moved from Nanny's apartment, and with Mr Brinkhoff's restored salary were able to rent a pleasant house in a tree-lined avenue to the east of Edvardplatz. They mourned the loss of their son but always kept their door open in the hope that Osbert would one day return to them.

Nanny was a changed woman. She was engaged to work for a family on Borgburg Avenue, looking after a beautiful and precocious little girl named Ingrid Van der Schmitt. But Nanny had learnt her lesson well. No more would she take her infant charges on trips to cemeteries or while away the hours discussing the deliciousness of a good murder. No, it was candy canes and china dolls and ribbons all the way. And Nanny hated it. It was enough to make her sick to her stomach.

'Do unto others before they can do unto you,' she croaked mournfully, gluing a picture of Osbert into her photograph album of favourite children.

And what of Isabella Myop? Every evening, as she practised at home on the Constantin Violin, she would remember what Mr Lomm taught her about inevitable musical outcomes, and the thought made her shiver.

A year had very nearly passed since Osbert's disappearance. One stormy night, the day before Isabella was due to return the Constantin Violin to the bank vaults of Muller, Baum and Spink, she entered her bedroom after supper to discover that the violin had gone. The shutters rattled noisily in the wind, beating so hard against the windowpanes she was sure the glass would shatter. Somebody had stolen the violin from her.

'It's Osbert,' insisted Isabella, her face even paler than usual. 'He came back to take the violin from me!'

'Nonsense,' said the Inspector of Police, who nursed a suspicion that Isabella had hidden the violin so she would never have to part with it. 'The boy's far away from Schwartzgarten now, or else he's dead.'

'You're perfectly safe, my darling angel,' trilled Mrs Myop hysterically. 'Nobody will come in the night to chop your pretty little head off.' She patted her terrified daughter's hand reassuringly. 'Nothing to worry about at all.'

But Isabella did worry. She worried so much that her pretty little head was no longer pretty at all; her face became grey and haunted, her features drawn and contorted. She could not sleep at night, and she often had the feeling she was being watched.

Mrs Myop would come to meet Isabella as she walked home from her school lessons with Mr Lomm above Salvator Fattori's delicatessen. Hurrying together along the frozen streets, Mrs Myop would tell Isabella dark tales, clutching her daughter's hand so tightly that Isabella's fingers turned white.

'Over rooftops little Osbert runs, with hair of flame and teeth like a wolf,' said Mrs Myop, gripping Isabella close at her side one ominously dark and icy night, a year to the day after Osbert's disappearance. 'He stands upon the chimney pots to play the violin and casts his shadow against the moon. Sometimes the music is so sad that the sky may crack.'

Isabella and her mother did not see Osbert's shadow against the wall.

'But it's just a story. There's nothing to fear, my darling angel,' said Mrs Myop, a distracted look in her eye. 'Osbert Brinkhoff won't trouble us again.'

But she was wrong. As Mrs Myop walked hand in

hand with Isabella, along the deserted street, Osbert stepped from the shadows and followed them into the night, his cleaver glinting in the moonlight.

Care to check out more ghastly goings-on in the city of Schwartzgarten?

Turn the page for today's late night edition of *The Informant*.

'FESTIVAL OF PRINCE EUGENE MUST PROCEED' DEMANDS PRINCIPAL

It was feared, in the light of recent murderous events, that the Festival of Prince Eugene would this year be abandoned. However, on the orders of the Principal of The Institute, The Informant is overjoyed to announce that the Festival will take place in accordance with traditions, to conclude with a grand display of fireworks above the carnival tent on Edvardplatz. Furthermore, the Governor of Schwartzgarten has declared that a reward of five hundred Imperial Crowns will be offered for information leading to the apprehension of the accursed Schwartzgarten Slayer. It is the earnest hope of The Informant that such a sum will be sufficient to bring an end to the Slayer's deadly rampage. It will gladden the hearts of the good citizens of Schwartzgarten to see the killer swiftly brought to trial and even more swiftly executed.

WHO IS THE SCHWARTZGARTEN SLAYER?

Is it safe to walk the streets alone? Will we be slaughtered as we sleep? It would seem to The Informant that the answer to the first question is a resounding 'no', and the answer to the second question is almost certainly a blood-curdling 'quite possibly'. How can the good citizens of Schwartzgarten go about their daily lives when the threat of murder and mayhem stalks them at every turn? It is vital that the Governor of Schwartzgarten should act - and act swiftly. If the Inspector of Police is not fit to the task of apprehending this murderous maniac, then a new Inspector must be appointed at once. Time is of the essence. No longer can we live in fear.

THE EDITOR

OLGA VAN VEENEN TO WRITE NEW BOOK?

It has been several years since the celebrated children's author Olga Van Veenen published her last book for children, *The Impossible Adventure*. Finally it seems that she is poised to begin writing a thrilling new work of fiction.

'It'll be a story about a boy,' says Miss Van Veenen, as I interview her over tea and macaroons at the Emperor Xavier Hotel. 'A boy with a bad temper, but a strong little boy who has many exciting and wonderful adventures.'

Why, I ask her, has it taken so long to put pen to paper? Miss Van Veenen laughs bravely, but in her eye there is an unmistakable twinkle of sadness.

'My heart aches, to think that I have kept my loyal army of children waiting,' says Miss Van Veenen as she feeds a morsel of pistachio macaroon to her treasured Pekingese Chou-Chou. 'I only hope that they will forgive their beloved Olga when they grasp my new book in their delightful little fingers.'

Any child wishing to become a member of the Van Veenen Adventure Society is encouraged to send his or her name and address in an envelope, enclosing one Imperial Crown, to: Claudius Estridge, Office 117 B, The Guild of Publishers and Printers, Alexis Street, Schwartzgarten.

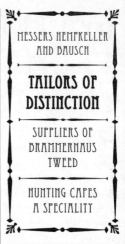

LETTERS FROM LUNATICS

The offices of The Informant have been deluged with letters and postcards, written in the scrawled and ill-disciplined handwriting of assorted lunatics and would-be wrongdoers, claiming responsibility for the Schwartzgarten Slayings. It is to be regretted that we cannot respond to each confession individually, but would encourage any genuine murderer or maniac to take themselves at once to the Department of Police, where they will be welcomed and processed with all due diligence.

The Black Museum of the Department of Police - Visitors by Appointment Only

The Black Museum houses many fascinating exhibits, including a guillotine blade (still stained with blood, from the time of Emeté Talbor), nooses large and small, an impressive assortment of wax heads of celebrated murderers and their victims, an absorbing collection of fingerprints and the most varied array of poison bottles outside that held in the collection of the University of Lüchmünster. The museum is not to be recommended for nervously predisposed parents or impressionable children.

THE
WOEBEGONE
TWINS

Turn the page for a sneak peek...

...If you dare.

CHAPTER ONE

— ◆·✕·◆ —

THE MORTENBERG twins stared out from the window of Aunt Gisela's kitchen. A man peered back at them, his piercing black eyes hooded by heavy grey lids. His head was unusually round and his skin had a wax-like pallor rarely seen on the face of a living creature.

'He's come to kill us,' whispered Feliks.

'Probably,' replied Greta. 'He looks the type that might.'

It was not unusual for the twins to expect the worst, nor was it entirely wrong for them to do so. From their earliest days they had been known as the Woebegone Twins, abandoned to their fate by disagreeable parents who preferred holidays in exotic climes and super-fast motorcars to spending time with their unfortunate offspring. Had it not been for Aunt Gisela, who had adopted the twins, they would have been brought up warped and peculiar within the foreboding walls of the

Schwartzgarten Reformatory for Maladjusted Children. Sometimes it is kinder to lie than to tell the truth, so Aunt Gisela had told the twins that their parents had died tragically in mysterious circumstances.

So the Woebegone Twins lived in Schwartzgarten with their aunt and her pet parrot, Karloff, in a warm and cheerful apartment in the grimmest, darkest part of the Old Town, across the street from Schroeder the Undertaker. When money was plentiful, Aunt Gisela would bake spiced gingerbread and her famous vanilla pudding. When times were hard, she would switch off the lights and sit inside her kitchen cupboard with the twins in her arms, hiding from the bailiffs.

The house always smelled of baking and beeswax and the aroma of Oil of Petunia, which Aunt Gisela dabbed liberally behind her ears every morning 'to keep away the moths'.

The twins had healthy appetites for the food that Aunt Gisela prepared for them. But there was one thing and one thing alone that they could not eat, and that thing was the humble almond nut. It was a discovery made early in their lives, when Aunt Gisela set to work baking the twins an almond marzipan torte on the occasion of their fifth birthdays. It was perhaps the most beautiful thing she had ever concocted: a towering confection of almond sponge cake with layers of almond marzipan and cloudberry jam, topped with glittering shards of almond nougatine.

'Eat up,' urged Aunt Gisela. 'You can eat the whole cake if you want, my hungry little monsters.'

The effect was instantaneous and dramatic. As soon as the twins sank their teeth into the moist, plump slices of almond cake, their tongues began to swell. And swell. And swell.

'Well, I wasn't expecting that,' said Aunt Gisela, telephoning for the doctor.

When Doctor Lempick arrived he examined the twins carefully. They were both deathly pale, and their tongues lolled from their mouths like deflated helium balloons.

'What I want to know is this,' said Aunt Gisela. 'What's happened to their tongues and will they be like that forever?'

Doctor Lempick smiled and shook his head. 'They

are allergic to almond nuts,' he concluded. 'Their tongues will return to normal size in due course. But please, never *ever* feed them another almond as long as they live.'

Apart from an allergy to almonds and the unfortunate disappearance of their parents, it would have seemed to the casual observer that the Mortenberg twins were entirely unremarkable. The only point of note was the striking similarity between the twins, although Greta was a little shorter and slightly stronger than her brother Feliks. Their hair was deep red, the colour of burnt barley sugar, and their pale faces were liberally scattered with freckles. But this hardly marked them out as extraordinary. If anything, it was Aunt Gisela who attracted most attention as she bustled along the cobbled streets of the Old Town with the twins in tow. Passers-by would often stop and stare at the woman, smiling with admiration and nodding as if at a fondly recalled memory.

'What are you staring at?' Aunt Gisela would shout, shaking her fist. 'Nothing better to do than gawp at old women who've done you no wrong?'

And though the twins often asked their aunt why she bawled and screamed at strangers in the street, she seemed deliberately vague on the subject.

Aunt Gisela's behaviour was curious at times, but her love for the twins was beyond doubt. So Greta and Feliks were happy to let their beloved aunt scream at whomsoever she wanted and were grateful for a roof over their heads.

But as the twins reached their eleventh birthdays, money was short and getting shorter and Aunt Gisela had no choice but to advertise for a boarder to rent a spare room in the apartment. And it was this boarder who now peered in through the window at the twins.

'That's him,' said Aunt Gisela. 'Our new house guest! Mr Morbide!'

She ran to the door and opened it wide.

'Mr Morbide!' cried Karloff from his cage. 'Mr Morbide!'

Morbide entered. He was a tall and bulky man and had to stoop to walk beneath the lintel. He was cloaked in a long black overcoat and carried a large suitcase and a small leather bag.

'Come in, come in!' cried Aunt Gisela, giving the man a crafty wink as she led him into the kitchen.

'Good evening,' growled Morbide in a voice so low that the teacups trembled in the rack above the sink.

The Woebegone Twins gasped and took a step backwards.

Feliks was quite certain that he saw a beetle drop from inside the man's overcoat and scuttle off across the tiled floor.

'Pull up a chair and eat,' commanded Aunt Gisela, grabbing a pan from the stove. 'Eat.'

Morbide sat at the table, but did not remove his coat. The twins stared hard at the man, who stared back at them and grunted. He reached into his pocket and retrieved a calling card, which he slid across the table to Greta.

The name 'Morbide' was embossed on the card, as if written in dripping blood.

'Well, sit down,' barked Aunt Gisela cheerfully at the twins. 'Duck eggs all round!'

The twins did as they were told and sat, hardly daring to breathe. They ate in silence.

One thing seemed certain to Greta: Morbide had murder on his mind.

DARK LORD

The Roald Dahl
FUNNY PRIZE
2012
Winner
booktrust

DARE TO READ ANOTHER TALE OF DARK DELIGHTS!

A WORK OF EVIL GENIUS BY ME

DARK LORD
THE TEENAGE YEARS

DIRK LLOYD
JAMIE THOMSON

978 1 40831 511 8 £5.99 Pbk
978 1 40831 655 9 £5.99 eBook

YOU CAN'T CALL ME A MONSTER

DARK LORD
A FIEND IN NEED

DIRK LLOYD
JAMIE THOMSON

978 1 40831 512 5 £5.99 PB Mar 2012
978 1 40831 656 6 £4.99 eBook Mar 2012

ORCHARD

www.orchardbooks.co.uk